Jamie Sedgwick
Published by Timber Hill press

Also by Jamie Sedgwick

Aboard the Great Iron Horse
The Clockwork God
Killing the Machine
The Dragon's Breath
Clockwork Legion
Starfall

Hank Mossberg, Private Ogre
Murder in the Boughs
Death in the Hallows
The Killer in the Shadow
A Fool There Was
When the Boughs Break
A Dame to Die For

Shadow Born Trilogy
Shadow Born
Shadow Rising

Shadowlord

The Tinkerer's Daughter
The Tinkerer's Daughter
Tinker's War
Blood and Steam

Standalone
The Darkling Wind
A Fool There Was

Watch for more at www.jamiesedgwick.com.

Table of Contents

Chapter 1 1
Chapter 2 13
Chapter 3 27
Chapter 4 31
Chapter 5 45
Chapter 6 57
Chapter 7 75
Chapter 8 87
Chapter 9 105
Chapter 10 117
Chapter 11 125
Chapter 12 139
Chapter 13 153
Chapter 14 167
Chapter 15 183
Chapter 16 203
Chapter 17 219
Chapter 18 231
A note from the author: 237

Chapter 1

A fool there was and he made his prayer
to a rag and a bone and a hank of hair
We called her the woman who did not care,
But the fool, he called her his lady fair.
  - Kipling

Allow me to introduce myself: I'm Sam Snyvvle, private investigator, goblin extraordinaire. I'm the undercity's only *true* private detective. There are imitators, but don't let them fool you. I'm the real deal. It may sound like I'm bragging, but I'm not. I'm just that good.

Got a problem? I'm your goblin. I'll take any case that comes my way. I find lost items, missing persons, catch cheating spouses and swindling business partners. For the right fee, a whole lot more.

But what's a goblin, you ask? Well, if you've read any fairy tales, I look pretty much like you'd expect: dark green skin, pointed ears, crooked nose, black claw-like nails and beady green eyes. And I'm about three feet tall. Hey, I'm not pretty. I know it. I have other strengths.

Like all goblins, I know what I want when I see it. I usually get it. So I stretch the truth now and then, maybe even get a little violent. At least I know how to get things done. The other races look down on us goblins because we tend to be sarcastic, sneaky, and morally flexible, but if you ask me, they're just jealous. With all their smug superiority, not one of them can best a goblin in a business deal. If you can't win at business, you might as well quit life. Am I right?

See, that's where goblins really shine. *Money.* Take a look at me, for example. I may just be a private dick, but I've got a place in the Hallows, not far from the docks and I even own a cabin up north, outside the undercity. I don't have the money to run out and buy a mansion up on Snob Hill or anything like that, but I do okay. I've even been thinking about getting a secretary. (Not that I really have any paperwork. I just like somebody soft and feminine around to pinch now and then.)

So I have my weaknesses; what can I say? *I'm a goblin.*

My biggest weakness is gambling. I like nothing better than a nice bloody prizefight. You win a few, you lose a few, but at least you know you're not the only one whose gonna get bloodied. I try not to bet on the fights too much. Fighting's a dirty business, and I'm not just talking about broken noses and brain damage. I'm talking about undercity mafia, the mob. The criminals who own the cops and just about everything else in the undercity, including the boxing ring and the fighters inside of it.

Anyway, speaking of boxing, that's exactly where I'd been on the Friday night *she* walked into my office. I had just returned from the *Palazio Straga* downtown. That's *Sharizi*, goblin-speak, for "Wizard's Palace." A lot of businesses in the undercity have goblin names. That's because most of them are owned by goblins. My race tends to be highly capitalistic. You

A FOOL THERE WAS

might say business is in our blood. You might also say criminal behavior and dishonesty are in our blood. I won't take offense. I've heard it all before.

It was a decent fight. Freddie "the Fist" Churchill took the prize in the fifth by a knockout. I forget the name of the guy he K.O.'d, and so had everybody else who put money on the chump. By morning, he'd just be another hobgoblin with a bruised ego and a minor concussion looking for a job. The rest of us would be looking for a way to make up the rent money we lost on him.

After the fight, I drove straight to my place on Wyvern Street at the north end of the Hallows. It's a condo in an old brick building, similar to a brownstone. It's not the greatest neighborhood. The place is run down and humid, like most everything in the undercity. There's so much moss and ivy on the outside of the building that you can hardly see the bricks.

Still, it ain't bad. I have a view looking out over the Bazaar, which means I've got easy access to all the trouble a goblin could ever want. The Bazaar is a trading place, a swap meet of sorts. You can get anything there, from an enchanted toaster to a dimebag of pixie dust. It's a good spot for a business like mine. Downtown, folks don't like to be seen talking to a private eye. In the Hallows, they can come and go as they please because nobody cares.

But I digress. This story isn't about the Hallows, it's about *her*.

I got home just after two a.m. and went straight upstairs to my office. I threw my wet raincoat over the rack by the door. The place was dark and musty, and it smelled like mildew and old cigars. I opened the curtains facing the street and the pale yellow light of the gas lamps came pouring in. That's more than enough light for a greenskin like me. My eyes are sharp as a raven's, and a trickle of starlight is all it takes to see clear as day, even on the darkest night.

I stood there a minute, gazing out at the fog and the drizzle, hypnotized by the reflections of the gas lamps on the cobblestones. I could still hear the roar of the crowd echoing in the back of my head and I couldn't help but wonder what it might have been like inside that ring. I've always wanted to be big and strong like Freddie the Fist; always dreamed of what it might be like to knock somebody out with a single punch, to have people afraid of me just because of the way I look. That must be quite a feeling. No, it's more than just a feeling. It's power, that's what it is. And goblins *crave* power. It's in our genetics.

Alas, nature's deck of cards threw me a different hand. I'm not big, even by goblin standards. I'm a quick thinker though, and I've got a mean streak a mile wide.

For any other kid my size, school might have been tough. He might have been bullied and pushed around, beaten up by the bigger, tougher kids. Not me. I was always quick with a joke and handy with a deck of cards. In fact, when it comes to gambling, I'm good at pretty much everything. The bullies may have been robbing the smaller kids at lunchtime, but they were losing it to me at the table in the back alley. And I was smart enough to keep a portion of that money to pay the biggest kid of all for his protection.

Think ahead. That's the key to success in any venture.

I settled into the old armchair at my desk and it squeaked like a trapped rat trying to climb out of a moldy dumpster. I

A FOOL THERE WAS

reached into the top drawer and pulled out a bottle of *Witch's Brew No. 3* and a shot glass. The old hag on the label wore a tall pointy hat and black cape, and she was stirring her cauldron with a long wooden paddle while flames and smoke rose up around her. The witch's familiar, a sleek black cat, was peeking out at me from under the edge of the label where the corner had peeled away from the bottle.

I poured a drink and threw it back in a hurry. Like all good booze, the 180 proof hickory-aged hooch burned all the way down. It brought a smile to my face and stirred up that warm feeling in my gut that I'd been longing for all night. I poured another, and then lit up a cigar and propped my feet up on the desk. I took a puff and blew a big oily smoke ring towards the ceiling.

So those are my weaknesses: prizefights, gambling, booze and good cigars. But I'd forgotten about the other one, until she knocked on my door. The sound shook me out of my trance, and I drew my gaze from the shot glass to the frosted window on the door bearing the inscription *"Sam Snyvvle, Private Investigator"* in big black letters.

I saw the unmistakable shapely silhouette of a tall beauty standing there and I had to fight my hereditary urge to clean the desk and slick back my hair. Goblins are, after all, a matriarchal society. We aren't just ruled by females, we're *dominated* by them. Nothing turns a goblin male to jelly faster than a beautiful woman. Hell, beauty isn't even necessary as long as the plumbing's all where it should be. I guess it has something to do with pheromones or hormones or some other 'ones that science hasn't discovered yet.

JAMIE SEDGWICK

I reminded myself to stay cool. She was probably there on business. Of course she was, why else would a woman come to my office? If there's one thing that can overcome a goblin's hormones it's the sweet *cha-ching* of currency, be it the gold coins preferred in the undercity or good old cash that flows down from San Francisco, topside. I'll even take Paypal, as long as your address is verified.

The undercity, in case you're wondering, is an ancient fairy city that was magically transported to a cavern underneath San Francisco during the industrial revolution. The oldest part of the undercity was originally located in the Mediterranean, where it was known as Vaneveh. It has been called by other names, but goblins have always known it as Baliztra ta'el mooka, *the City of Fools.* That's because it's the place to go to if you're looking to sell a bridge or host a card game. There's no shortage of suckers in the undercity, and if there's any one rule that all goblins abide by, it's this: *All fools must be separated from their cash.*

"Door's open," I said, taking another puff on my cigar. In stepped a tall, sultry, blonde-haired vixen wearing a slightly damp fur coat and a long red dress. I recognized her immediately. Her name was Honey. She was a singer. In fact, she wasn't just any singer, she was the star attraction at a nightclub downtown where I'd spent many long nights and many hundreds of dollars on overpriced booze, dreamily watching her stroll back and forth through the crowd, hoping I'd be the one whose lap she'd land on.

I wasn't the only one. Honey was a dryad with just enough human blood to put a little meat on her bones. She was a

A FOOL THERE WAS

goddess. A goddess in high heels and a red dress. A real life femme fatale. Crazy sexy.

I stared at her, mouth agape, cigar dangling from my lower lip as Honey set her umbrella by the door and removed her coat, exposing the pale translucent skin of her arms and throat. She wore the glistening skin-tight red dress from her act, a long elegant evening gown that somehow managed to be both classy and pornographic all at once. She knelt down to adjust the straps on her heels and glanced over her shoulder at me with a sultry smile.

I played it cool, pretending I hadn't been staring at her in the way we both knew I had. I wasn't worried. If she hadn't wanted me to take a peek, she wouldn't have made it so easy. She's a dame. That's how they think.

"Mr. Snyvvle, I presume," she said, straightening up.

I blew a puff of smoke in her direction. "Call me Sam. You're Honey, right?"

She smiled. Her gaze flickered to some distant place no one else could see. "Honey is my stage name. My real name is Brigette. Brigette Love. Your cigar stinks, Mr. Snyvvle."

I doused it in the ashtray. I know what's good for business, and for romance, too. I rose to my feet and offered to shake her hand. She accepted gracefully, with a touch as cool and soft as a cloud. I glanced up into her hazel eyes and knew exactly why her name was Love. It may as well have been Aphrodite. I was smitten.

"Have a seat," I said, pulling myself together as well as I could. "What can I do for you, Ms. Love?"

She settled into the chair across from me and crossed her legs. Her dress parted, revealing enough of her thigh that I felt like I should be putting a dollar bill in her garter. I poured another shot of *Witch's Brew*. I offered it to her, and she declined.

"This is a delicate matter," she said, ignoring my straying glance at her unbelievably long legs. "I assume you can be trusted with confidentiality?"

"Like your own mother. I'll go to the grave before spilling your secrets." I meant it, too. Not necessarily for *everyone,* but I meant it for her.

"That's very comforting, Mr. Snyvvle-"

"Sam."

"Sam. Thank you. The issue at hand is a rare and valuable gem. It's something precious that was stolen from me, and I'd like it back."

"I see. Can you describe this gem?"

"Yes. It's called the Scarlet Tear. It's the third largest pink diamond ever found. Fifty carats, to be exact."

I whistled. "I see. And when did it go missing?"

"Three days ago."

I stroked my long narrow chin, feeling the stubble bite into my fingertips. "You realize that the thief may be long gone by now?" I said. "A rock like that must be worth millions, and no half-sane crook would stick around with it for long."

"Fifteen million," she said matter-of-factly. "Twenty perhaps, but don't worry about that. I know exactly where it is. In fact, it's just across town, right now."

"How do you know that?"

"Because I already know who stole my diamond, Mr. Snyvvle. The problem is not in finding the thief; it's in getting him to return my property."

A FOOL THERE WAS

I had a sinking feeling that there was a lot more to the story. I knew right then that I should've kicked her out of there with a fare-thee-well kick in the ass. Alas, it's not my way. I rarely turn down a job and I *never* turn down a beautiful woman. I sighed.

"Who stole it?" I said.

"Pretty Boy Marcozi."

"So that's what it sounds like when the other shoe drops."

"Please Sam, don't give up on me yet," she said in a pleading voice.

"Stop it, you're gonna make me cry."

"Don't you understand that you're my last hope? If you won't help me, I just don't know what I'll do."

"What do you want from me?" I said. "Getting killed isn't gonna get you that rock."

Pretty Boy Marcozi is one of the city's biggest crime lords. He's *kindred,* a mix of goblin and human blood that gave him the exotic good looks for which he was nicknamed. He looks mostly human, but with long pointed ears, pale moss-colored skin, and deep green hair.

Marcozi owns a high-rise downtown known as Pixieland. The place has it all: shopping mall, movie theater, even a swimming pool. The higher levels are business offices and luxury apartments. Marcozi lives on the top floor. He rents the other levels to some of the richest and most powerful fairy creatures in the world.

Honey leaned forward across my desk, her platinum bangs falling teasingly over her eyes. Her dress dangled low in the front, offering a spectacular view of the Sierras.

"Go to him, Sam. Tell him to give it to me. Make him-"

"Make him!" I blurted. "You want me to *make* Pretty Boy Marcozi give up that diamond? You realize he's the most notorious gangster in the city? He could have us both killed as easily as snapping his fingers."

"I know that Sam, but I *must* have my diamond back. See, Dave and I -that's Pretty Boy's real name, Dave- we were dating for a while. A few days ago, I broke it off with him and he didn't like it so well. He stole my diamond. But I need it, Sam. I need to sell it, because if I don't I'll never get out of that club. I want to have *children*. I want to get married. I'd do *anything* to get that diamond back!"

At this point, she was practically lying across my desk and I nearly had my long bony nose stuck somewhere between Mount Shasta and Mount Rainier. Only I wasn't staring down there anymore. I was lost in her eyes. My heart was pounding, the crowd was cheering, and I was Freddie the Fist, and it was glorious.

"I'll pay you," she added, almost as an afterthought. "Cash, gold, whatever you want. I'll make you the richest goblin in the undercity. All you have to do is say *Yes*."

"All right," I said. The crowd went wild. Honey bent closer, her cleavage straining against the fabric in a way that would've killed a lesser goblin. She reached out to stroke my chin and her voice dropped to a near whisper:

"Thank you so much, Sam. You don't know what this means to me. I'll do anything to repay you. Anything." She kissed me on the cheek, long and soft and moist, hot as the jungle in July. I cleared my throat.

"Right. Okay then. I, uh... I charge by the day... and something about expenses."

A FOOL THERE WAS

"Sure, baby. Anything. Just name your price and go get my diamond. Pretty Boy keeps it in a safe behind his desk. You can't miss it." She rose to her feet and straightened her dress. I studied her quietly, the words *"get my diamond"* ringing in my ears like the sound of the bell as Freddie the Fist's opponent hit the mat.

I'd been Freddie for a minute there. Now I was the guy bleeding on the floor. I didn't know how it had happened.

Chapter 2

I threw on my coat and hat and walked Honey down to the street where a cab was waiting for her. I offered her a ride home, but she smiled and said it was time to go back to work. Then the cab took off and I stared after it, watching the tiny red halos of the brake lights vanish into the mist, wondering why a woman like Honey Love needed money bad enough to come to a guy like me.

"Here's another fine mess you've gotten yourself into, you damned fool," I muttered into the fog.

I didn't believe all Honey's talk about getting out of show biz and starting a family. I'd seen her act. Honey knew what she was doing, and she did it well. I was sure she made a decent living at it. Any woman who can draw a crowd like Honey does, doesn't have to worry about money.

She was lying to me. The whole scene in my office had been an act, a way to get me to do what she wanted. But that didn't stop me from wanting to do it anyway. I don't know, maybe I thought I had a chance with Honey because she had come to me and not somebody else. Maybe I was thinking about how grateful she'd be when I handed her that diamond. Maybe I was even thinking of keeping that diamond for myself.

A chunk of rock that size can buy a lot of Honeys...

Regardless, it was time for me to go to work. It was still early (about two-thirty a.m.) and there was no reason for me not to start working on the case right away. I had four hours until sunrise. That was plenty of time to look into the situation. At least I'd have a better idea of what I was getting into.

I wasn't sure how I was going to get to Pretty Boy Marcozi, but I had a pretty good idea how he'd react when I asked him for that diamond. I didn't have to think too hard to know I couldn't go about things that way. Even if I could talk my way into the upper floors of his building and somehow get face to face with him, there was no way Pretty Boy would hand that stone over. Thankfully, I had other options. For a clever goblin, there are always other options.

I opened the door of my '29 Ford and nearly plopped down into a pool of water. I groaned as I realized I'd left the window cracked open and the rain had been splashing inside for the last hour. One thing about old cars is they don't take the weather too well. If you don't keep 'em dry, they'll rust faster than a nail in a can of cola. And if there's one thing in my life I take care of, it's my car. I hurried back upstairs to get a towel.

As you may have guessed, cars are another one of my weaknesses. An old hot rod with a souped-up engine and a thick glossy coat of paint is a thing of beauty. I love the smell of burning gasoline, the rumble of a big block engine, and the flash of fire that shoots out the tailpipe when you really give it the gas.

My '29 doesn't have any flames painted on her or anything like that, just a sleek candy apple red paint job with a chopped top, step rails, and a supercharged big-block V8 with no hood,

A FOOL THERE WAS

so you can drool enviously all over the engine. Just don't touch her, or I'll make your hands into hood ornaments.

After drying the seat, I fired her up. She started on the first try, as always. Nothing in the world is more reliable than a Chevy engine in a Ford chassis.

I headed for the highway, or the closest thing we have to it in the undercity. Baliztra has one major road that creeps around the lake and connects to just about every major neighborhood, from the skyscrapers Downtown to the Wells at the south end of the cavern. Problem is, it's just a two-lane road and traffic is a nightmare.

Sure, tons of creatures in the undercity can fly, but folks still need to haul groceries around, take the kids to school, and that's not counting the tens of thousands of kindred who are mostly human but have enough fae blood to live in the undercity.

If you ask me, I think we should kick 'em all out. The kindred, that is. It's hard enough finding places to live in the modern world without inviting the zebras down from topside. That's what we call humans: *zebras,* 'cause they mostly come in two flavors: dark or light.

Can you imagine that? In Baliztra, we've got every color of the rainbow, with or without fur, and you can throw in a set of wings here and a tail there for good measure. Greenskins, brownskins, grays, blues... it's all pretty much the same for the fae. We're just a freak show that never ends.

Being a weekend, I didn't run into too much traffic. I made it downtown in twenty minutes and parked at the garage between Fairyblooms and Elvendales, a few blocks from Pixieland. I always make it a habit to park at a safe distance when I'm doing things of questionable legality. That way, if I get made, I can still get to my car before anyone finds it. Also, it leaves the coppers one less piece of evidence at the scene of the crime.

I walked the short distance to Pixieland and then waltzed in the front doors like a regular customer. I got *the look* from two hobgoblin guards sizing me up at the door, but I ignored them. Ain't no law against shopping. If they wanted to do something about it, I had a magic ring in my pocket that could hit like a truckload of brass knuckles. If that didn't work, I had a taser handy, too.

I also have a magic wand, and I don't mean the one I'm saving for the ladies. It's a nice wand made of copper and brass tubing with a two-inch crystal at the end. I keep that in the glove box. Casting spells isn't a strong point for goblins. I never was much good at it. I do have some hereditary tricks however, and they come in handy from time to time. Like the ability to start fires with my mind. Just little ones, mind you, but one tiny, well-placed fire can grow rather large quite fast.

I also have a knack for hiding things. That's because goblins are hoarders, like packrats. We notice all the tiny little cracks and crevices that are in plain sight, yet somehow invisible to people who aren't paying attention. This skill also gives me an advantage when it comes to finding things that are lost or stolen. That's why I'm such a natural at P.I. work.

I took the escalator up to the fourth level, through the mall and the shopping center, and that was as far as I could go without a badge. Beyond that, you have to go through security to prove you either work or live up in the higher levels. That is, unless you've got a key to the private elevator at the back of

A FOOL THERE WAS

the building. I didn't, but my philosophy is that anything that requires a key *can* be opened without one.

I stood at the railing for a minute, taking inventory of the place. A thousand fae creatures surrounded me. Elves, brownies, dwarves, centaurs, you name it. Most of the security goons were hobgoblins. They're a crossbreed between goblins and field giants, the little ones. Hobgoblins stand about seven feet tall. They're built like professional wrestlers, they have nasty dispositions, and they're not too smart, which makes them perfect for security and police jobs. They can be told what to do with no worries that they'll try thinking for themselves. And they don't mind breaking bones. In fact, they live for it.

There were at least half a dozen guards roaming each level of the place, and many more hanging out in the shops and stores. Two of the goons walked right past me and continued on their way without a backwards glance. As soon as they were out of sight, I zigzagged through the crowd and made a beeline for the tall white door marked "Private" that stood between a coffee shop and an Apple store. Yeah, we've got those in the undercity, too. Freaks love Apple.

The door wasn't locked, so I slipped inside and found myself in a brightly illuminated hallway with black and white checkered tiles on the floor and an endless green stripe painted on one wall. Everything else was white, glaringly bright. The overall effect was dizzying. I hesitated a moment, wondering if I'd accidentally swallowed one of those hallucinogenic toadstools that the delver-dwarves like so much.

I shook my head, wondering what sort of manic fae creature would dream up that color scheme. It had to be a fairy,

I thought. But who the hell would hire a fairy as their interior decorator? The mind boggles.

I scurried down the hall, senses alert for any sign of danger. I reached the corner and turned left, and the hallway opened up like a maze before me. Doorways and hallways branched off left and right, as far as the eye could see. I noticed the glare of elevator doors in the distance, and smiled. I hurried in that direction, already fumbling in my pockets for my lock-picking kit.

By the time I reached the doors, I had my kit open and my second-favorite tool in hand. I glanced back and forth, making sure no one else was coming, and then knelt down to pick the lock. The system had an electronic card scanner, the kind that opens the door automatically when the computer reads the radio tag imprinted inside the card. I know ways around that system, but they're time consuming. I didn't bother.

The control panel had a steel lock to allow maintenance workers to open it up for repairs. I noted the generic name stamped onto the faceplate of the lock and grinned. I jammed the tension wrench into place and stuck the pick all the way in. I pulled, testing the pins for resistance. I tackled them one at a time, using pressure on the tension wrench to identify the order of the pins. It took all of four seconds to open the lock. I pulled the panel open and found myself staring at a command console with a tiny L.E.D. readout.

"This is too easy," I said.

I hit the "Open Door" key and a spark went off. The shrill scream of a siren cut through the air. A recessed speaker in the ceiling overhead buzzed to life and a female voice said:

A FOOL THERE WAS

"Intruder Alert! Intruder Alert! Code Seventeen, Level Four, Section Nine!"

I stepped back, wondering where the hell I'd gone wrong. That was when I noticed the vague imprint of elven script at the top of the panel, revealed by the soot in the puff of smoke. *Crap*. Elven magic. Somebody had cast a protection spell on the elevators, and I'd set it off by tampering with the lock. I jammed my kit back into my pocket and looked left and right, considering my next move. That was when the door crashed open at the end of the tunnel and I heard someone shout:

"He's this way!"

I glanced back and forth, contemplating ducking down another hallway or hiding in a janitor's closet. That was no good, I realized. Every door in the place was bound to be locked, and if I went racing down one of those tunnels, I'd probably end up right in the arms of a squad of hobgoblins. Even if I did make it out of there, I'd never get back inside, and that wasn't acceptable. I hadn't come this far for nothing.

I hit the "Open Door" button again, and nothing happened. The computer had locked me out. Frantically, I started pressing all of the buttons, hoping to short-circuit the system. That didn't work, either. I heard a shout and turned my head just in time to see two massive hobgoblins come barreling around the corner behind me. They were going so fast that they slid on the tiles as they rounded the corner and slammed into the wall. They went down in a heap. I heard the guy on the bottom grunt loudly.

"Get off me, moron!" he shouted. I saw his fist appear out of nowhere. He decked the second guard right between the eyes. He grunted and rolled to the side.

I frantically dug through my trench coat pockets, looking for my magic ring. My hands closed on my car keys, my lock-picking kit, and then something soft and squishy that I'd probably been saving for a snack until I forgot about it. I checked my trousers. Nothing in the left pocket... ah, at last! I sighed like Frodo in a bar fight as my fingers closed on the ring. I pulled it out, shoved it onto the middle finger of my right hand, and then punched the control panel as hard as I could.

There was an explosion of smoke and light. A thick black cloud rolled up towards the ceiling, and the scent of burning plastic filled my nostrils. The elevator doors slid open. A pleasant female voice said: "Welcome!"

"Thanks," I grumbled.

The hobgoblins were back on their feet and barreling towards me like a freight train with no brakes. I heard a shout and turned, only to realize that a second pair of guards was closing in on me from behind. I closed my fist, feeling the weight of the ring, wondering if I had any chance whatsoever of coming out of there alive.

I turned, glancing back and forth in each direction as the two groups closed in on me. I couldn't help but wince, imagining what they'd do to me if they got their hands on me.

Like I said before, I'm not that big. These guys could break my bones like toothpicks. I wanted to duck and run, but I couldn't. I knew I'd never get away. I had to do something else: I had to outsmart them. So I waited. I stood there in breathless anticipation, knowing full well that when they hit me I'd squish like a frog under the tire of my hot rod. I fought the cowardly urge to run for my life, because I knew there was nowhere to go. I tried to focus.

A FOOL THERE WAS

Think of money, I told myself. *Truckloads and truckloads of cash!*

They closed in on me and the floor rattled under my feet like the tracks of the undercity subway tram. Then, at the very last second, an instant before they pulverized me into a puddle of green snot, I stepped backwards into the elevator.

Just as I'd expected, the hobgoblins were too stupid to react. Even if they'd had the reflexes, they were still going too fast. With the sound of a dump truck crashing into a ravine, they slammed into each other at full speed. For a second, their bodies seemed to compress into one single solid mass: a creature made of arms, legs, flashlights and blue trousers. Then they hit the floor with a rumble and a whole lot of shouting. Before they could even move, I reacted.

I leapt out of the elevator and hit the guy on top of the pile as hard as I could, right in the forehead. My ring worked its magic. His head snapped back. His eyes rolled up as the imprint of my ring turned into a red horizontal stripe across his forehead. He went limp. The other guards grunted and moaned as the full weight of his body pressed down on the hobgoblins beneath him.

I hopped back into the elevator and pressed the button for the top level. Then, just as the doors closed, I reached out and snagged a keychain from one of the guard's belts.

I felt myself rising into the air, and the pleasant sounds of Kenny G came rolling out of the speakers. I smiled and tucked my ring back into my pocket. I began thumbing through the keys. I wasn't sure if I'd need them or not, but I *was* sure they'd come in handy some other time. *Think ahead!*

JAMIE SEDGWICK

Half a minute later, the elevator came to a gentle rest. I stood near the back wall, the fingers of my right hand doing a tap dance on the grip of the taser hanging from the back of my belt. I didn't have much of a plan. If there were guards waiting for me, I was going to shoot and run, and hope I made it through.

Thankfully, that wasn't necessary. The bell chimed, the doors opened, and I found myself staring into the doorway of Pretty Boy's flat. The news of my break-in must not have reached the top floor yet, because the place was quiet and dark. I stepped into the hallway and the lights automatically came up. The doors slid shut behind me, and the jazzy sounds of Freita Garble came drifting out of the ceiling.

Pretty Boy's front door was a heavy-duty steel contraption, the kind you might expect a crime lord to have. The strange thing was that the door was standing wide open. That in itself should have worried me. I assumed it was because Pretty Boy was home, and possibly expecting company. That would explain how I'd made it that far so easily.

Pretty Boy was nowhere in sight, so I stepped inside and quietly closed and locked the door behind me. I figured that would buy me a few minutes when the security guards caught up with me. I stood there a moment, taking it all in.

Pretty Boy's flat was a mansion on top of a skyscraper. The kitchen was off to my right and the living room to my left. In front of me, a long wall of windows looked out over the city and across the lake, all the way to *The Estates* up on Snob Hill. It was the kind of view most of us only get if we're born with wings. Pretty Boy had something better than wings. He had money.

A FOOL THERE WAS

The place was tastefully furnished with contemporary stainless steel appliances and chairs, and plenty of wrought iron lights hanging from the ceiling. Paintings and art pieces decorated the living room. Many of them I recognized. Most appeared to be original, and a few were priceless.

Being absolutely fascinated with material wealth, most goblins are intimately familiar with things of great value. I'm no exception. I immediately noted the original Picasso hanging over the mantle. I remembered reading an article in the news a few years earlier. It had been stolen from some movie star living topside in San Francisco. Now I knew why it was never found.

Then there was the 1922 first edition of *Ulysses* sitting on the coffee table. A similar copy recently sold for a quarter of a million bucks. Or maybe it was the same one, considering the fact that there are only four in existence. Pretty Boy had an entire bookshelf of rare editions encased in glass. He'd vacuumed all the oxygen out, probably even pumped in some other inert gas that would prevent oxidation of the fragile paper. I was tempted to smash it open and pocket a few, along with half the other stuff in that room. Hell, just one of those paintings could retire me on a yacht.

Unfortunately, security had already seen me inside the building. If anything went missing, they'd tie it directly to me. Also, I had no doubt that Pretty Boy had installed some serious security to protect his belongings. I'd probably set alarms off the instant I touched something. That would be especially bad, since he was apparently in that apartment with me somewhere.

That thought was enough to get me moving. I lowered my stance and tiptoed across the room with the kind of stealth only two living beings possess: goblins and ninjas. Goblins of course, being the sneakier of the two. I hurried across the living room and down the hall, peering into the doorways that opened along the way. I passed a bathroom larger than my apartment and a library full of books and computers with a glowing blue waterfall that cascaded down into a koi pond.

The third door on the right was the office. That was where Honey had said I'd find the safe. The door was partially ajar, and I could hear noises coming from inside. That gave me pause. If Pretty Boy was in there, I'd have to find a way to lure him out so I could get to the safe.

I dropped to my knees and waited there a minute, the folds of my trench coat spreading out across the floor around me. I heard a rustling sound like the movement of fabric, followed by a brief silence. Then the sound came again, twice this time, and again the silence. I frowned. If I didn't know better, I'd have thought it was a curtain blowing in the breeze of an open window.

But what about Pretty Boy? If he wasn't in the office, then where was he? Security hadn't appeared yet, so I must not have set off any alarms. If the alarm system was off, that meant Pretty Boy was home. Didn't it?

I quietly placed a hand on the door and nudged it further open, just enough to peek inside. To the left I saw a massive fish tank and a tan leather sofa. I couldn't see much more than that. I took off my hat and leaned forward, craning my neck so I could see around the door. The desk appeared, and in the chair next to it, the corpse of Pretty Boy Marcozi.

I pushed the door open and stepped into the room. The window behind the desk was broken, and one of the curtains was flapping in the breeze. Every few seconds, a gust came up

A FOOL THERE WAS

and slapped the fabric against the chair with Pretty Boy's body. I stepped around the side of the desk to get a better look at his face.

It was Marcozi all right, reclining in his chair with a horrifying grimace and a bullet hole the size of a tennis ball through his chest. I checked my watch and noted the time. The bodies of fae creatures don't last too long after death. Within a few hours, they crumble into a fine golden dust. Pretty Boy wasn't full-blooded, though. He was kindred, and that meant his human blood could make his body last much longer. Possibly even weeks.

I couldn't discern anything about his time of death, so I stepped closer for a better look at the bullet hole. Already, something didn't make sense. Guns are for humans. Most fae can't even shoot a gun because of our light bone structure. Not to mention the fact that we can accomplish the same ends using magic. Why make a big bloody mess with a gun, when you can just as easily wave your wand? Not to mention the fact that guns are noisy, and therefore bound to attract attention. The whole thing was bizarre.

I scanned the area around the body, looking for clues. There was no sign of a struggle. Pretty Boy had been working on a ledger of some sort, but a quick glance told me it was just standard bookkeeping stuff. I was sure he had other ledgers worth killing for, but this wasn't one of them. The others would be in the safe.

At the corner of the desk, I saw a picture of Pretty Boy with an attractive violet-haired dryad. She looked part dryad, anyway. The way the fae blood mixes around here, it can get confusing sometimes. I flipped it over and took a gander at the notation on the back of the photo. It said: *Dave and Nyva Marcozi, 2014*

I stepped around the body and looked at the painting on the wall. It was an old watercolor of a roman solarium with a half-nude woman on a couch. It wasn't anything special, which was a tipoff right there. In a house full of Picassos and first editions, this was something designed *not* to attract attention. I pulled on it, and the painting swung away on a hinge, revealing a safe hidden in the wall. Strangely, the safe was already open. I pulled the door wide, revealing a stack of cash, a tray full of gold coins, and a small ledger bound in black leather. What I didn't see was the very thing I had come for in the first place.

The diamond was gone.

Somewhere in the distance, I heard a voice shout: "Marcozi, are you in there? It's the police. If you don't open the door, we'll break it down!"

Chapter 3

My life began in a narrow little alley behind a tiny Italian restaurant in The Wells. That's another district in the undercity, similar to The Hallows, but classier. I was born in a wooden milk crate. That may not sound like much, but it's standard fare in the goblin world. In fact, Mom -whoever she may have been- was kind enough to fill the box with shredded paper and cotton stuffing from an old mattress before she squatted down and emptied her swollen womb.

Then she left us, forever.

I can't say I blame her. Baby goblins are hideous things. Big, swollen eyes, soft green fur and erect little puppy dog ears, like some sort of house pet. We even make these awful, cute little *cooing* noises. Gag me already. I wouldn't blame her if she'd grabbed the nearest brick and smashed our gooey little brains out. No wonder I hate kids.

I was the runt of the bunch. I was the smallest, and the last to gain consciousness. I woke to the sound of my biggest, meanest brother sharpening a Spork into a makeshift shiv against a piece of brick. My eyes fluttered open, and I found myself in the shadowy corner of the box, buried under the stuffing and shredded paper. I moved my head slightly so that I could see what was going on, and in the process revealed myself. I instantly realized my mistake. The second I moved, my brother turned in my direction and fixed me with a malicious glare.

I glanced around the crate and saw two of my siblings already lying dead on the floor. The corpse of another lay draped over the back of the box. I looked at the goblin, and the corners of his mouth curled up in an evil grin. I gulped.

See, when a litter of goblins is born, the first thing they do is start killing each other. It's in our nature. Call it the *struggle for survival*, or *survival of the fittest*. Whatever. What it boils down to is the fact that the world has a finite amount of resources, and goblins are genetically programmed to protect their own interests. The sooner we take out the competition, the more likely we are to survive. The better you are at surviving, the more likely you'll end up wealthy and powerful, and that's the way the game is played. That's why we're so good at it. Because it's an *instinct*.

The goblin tossed the brick aside as I crawled to my feet. He tested the sharpened blade on his tongue, making a long slice that instantly drew blood. He licked it off the blade and swirled it in his mouth, savoring it like fine wine. Then he raised the shiv and lunged at me.

I latched onto the edge of the box in a desperate attempt to climb out of reach, and the sharpened Spork *whizzed* past me, grazing my arm as the goblin embedded it into the wall of the box. I instantly lost my grip and fell flat on my back. I pushed up on my hands, crab-walking backwards through the paper shreds as my brother struggled to remove the shiv from the soft wood. He put a foot up on the board and yanked it free.

A FOOL THERE WAS

I was halfway across the crate as he turned around and came at me for the second time. I grabbed a handful of paper shreds and tossed them in his face. He instinctively threw up a hand and snarled. I used that time to roll over and lunge towards the wall. I had learned from my first mistake.

I caught onto the ledge this time, and I didn't let go. My toenails and claws dug into the wood as I pulled myself up. My arms shook with the effort, but I forced myself to keep moving. I pulled myself up high enough to prop an elbow on the ledge and began swinging my leg, trying to bring it up and over. At that point, big bro was just an arm's length away.

Just as my leg went up over the ledge, I caught a movement in the corner of my eye. I swung my head around and saw another goblin outside the crate. He was lunging at me with a long wooden shish-kebab skewer. I released my grip and dropped to the cobblestones, flat on my back. The skewer missed me by an inch. It plunged through the slats in the milk crate and impaled big bro right through the shoulder.

He howled like a demon. The Spork-shiv fell to the floor, forgotten as he wrestled to free himself. He drew back into the far corner, taking the skewer with him. The second goblin raised a fist in the air and cheered at his success. With a roar, big brother pulled the skewer free. He spun it around and, with both hands, drove it right through the wall of the crate, and into our brother's ribs.

That ended the cheering. I didn't wait around to see what happened next. I hit the cobblestones at full speed and headed for the mouth of the alley. As luck would have it, another sibling appeared out of the shadows. This one was female, probably the only one in the litter, seeing as how rare female goblins are. She was armed with a broken beer bottle. I skidded to a stop and went scurrying back in the other direction as fast as my little legs could carry me. As I ran, I saw others emerging from the shadows.

They'd been hiding, stalking each other, waiting for the opportunity to kill. Being the runt, I made an easy mark, and my flight through the alley drew them all out of hiding. Before I knew it, I had the whole pack after me. A quick glance over my shoulder told me there were at least ten still alive. The odds were not in my favor.

I reached a wooden staircase halfway down the alley and began to climb, looking for safety in higher ground. As I reached the top step, the door swung open and light came flooding out. I stood to the side behind the door, with my back pressed up against the wall, my heart about to explode out of my chest.

"Gah! what's this?" a human's voice shouted. "Beat it, ya ratfinks!" A human-looking kindred man wearing an apron and a white chef's hat propped the door open and went charging after them with a broom. My brothers and sister scurried off in every direction, some of them disappearing into the trash, others fleeing the alley.

While he had them on the run, I slipped under the edge of the door and disappeared into the kitchen.

Chapter 4

When I heard the cops pounding on the front door, I flew into action. I stepped away from the safe and glanced around the room, trying to remember what I'd touched. I grabbed a tissue from the desk and quickly wiped the painting, the safe, and the photo of Pretty Boy and his wife Nyva.

Satisfied that I'd removed any traces of my presence in the room, I pulled open the curtains and glanced outside, looking for a possible escape route. No luck, just a smooth, sheer wall of concrete and glass. I took a deep breath, trying to calm my nerves.

That was when I realized that I was about to miss a golden opportunity. I rushed over to the safe, snatched up the ledger, and shoved it into my trench coat pocket. I was tempted to take more, but there was no way I could carry it all. The coins were too heavy and noisy, and the cash took up too much space. It didn't matter. The information in that ledger was worth a king's ransom. Besides, when the cops found the safe full of money, they'd have a heck of a time figuring the motive for Pretty Boy's murder. That was important, since they were going to come looking for me eventually. The less they could pin on me, the better.

As I raced down the hallway, I heard the sound of the cops hammering at the door, trying to bust it down. I paused to glance into each room that I passed. I was looking for a good hiding spot, maybe even a way to get into the crawlspace under the floor, or up in the ceiling. I reached the end of the hall and stepped into Pretty Boy's bedroom. It was impressive.

It was the size of a house, probably two thousand square feet in total. It had luxurious leather and hardwood furnishings, a walk-in shower with a dozen spray nozzles, a hot tub the size of a small swimming pool, and a television that took up an entire wall. I saw a poster bed that looked like it was carved from white marble, and a walk-in closet that was bigger than my office.

It was enough to make me wish I had the time to go over the place more thoroughly. Pretty Boy's flat was a literal treasure trove. Granted, he didn't exactly get all that through hard work and studious application. No, he did it the goblin way: by fighting, stealing, and murdering his way to the top. It was still impressive though, considering that all goblins start out pretty much the same.

I circled the room, trying to find a way out. I could hear the creaking sound of the front door's hinges down the hall. I knew I was down to my last few seconds. That door was about to give, and when it did, I'd be up to my eyeballs in blue uniforms. I pulled open the walk-in closet at the exact moment the front door exploded into the living room. I ducked inside and pulled the doors shut behind me.

I could hear shouting, the heavy footsteps of jackbooted thugs racing through the apartment. I blinked, hoping to gain my nightvision, but there was too much light streaming in through the slats in the doors. Having no other choice, I took a deep breath and summoned a spark of energy. A warm

A FOOL THERE WAS

sensation ran down my right arm, raising the hairs on my skin and making my nerves tingle. The charge quickly ramped up to a higher frequency, like tiny vibrations moving through my body. The speed and energy built rapidly towards an inevitable climax, and I snapped my fingers. A small flickering flame rose up from my index finger.

I held the flame aloft and scanned the interior of the closet, hoping to find some sort of crawlspace between floors. No such luck. There was no trapdoor anywhere in sight. The ceiling was solid gypsum board, and so were the walls. However, that realization gave me an idea. If the walls were thin enough, I might be able to break through without rousing anyone's attention. It might be messy, but it was better than going to prison.

I pushed aside the row of suits hanging at the back of the closet and gently rapped on the wall with my knuckle. A smile came to my lips as I heard the unmistakable hollow sound of dead space. I stepped closer, with the intention of bumping a test hole in the wall with my elbow. In my haste, I moved too quickly and blew out the flame.

I snapped it back to life, ignoring the heat that had been building up in my fingertip. If I allow the flame to burn long enough, I can get a blister, but at that moment, I didn't care. As the flame at my fingertip reignited, it grazed the edge of a dangling spider web. The web instantly flared into an inferno, and suddenly all I could see was a wall of flames.

A wave of heat washed over me. I threw my hands up to protect my face. I took a step, nearly tripping over my own feet in the process. Then, just as suddenly as it had started up, the fire burnt out, leaving me once again in almost total darkness.

My eyes had adjusted to the brightness of the flames by then, and I couldn't see a damned thing. I immediately tripped over a pair of shoes on the floor and went stumbling forward with all the grace of a drunken clown on a unicycle. I threw my arms out, latching onto the clothes that dangled down around me. They easily ripped away from their hangers and down I went.

My face slammed full-force into the back wall. I saw a flash of stars. I landed in a heap of clothes, and smacked my head solidly on the concrete floor. A meteor shower went off in my vision. For a few seconds I just lay there, blinking, wondering just how much noise I'd made. I expected the cops to come roaring in to collect me any second. What I didn't even realize was that I had inadvertently managed to pop open a hidden door in the wall.

I gradually came to my senses and found myself sprawled out in a narrow, dimly lit passageway. A spring-loaded mechanism inside the hidden door activated and tried to pull it shut. The door banged painfully against my knee. I heard voices in the bedroom, and realized that the cops were just a few feet away. I twisted aside, caught the door, and very slowly, very gently, let it slide back into place. With the slightest *click,* it locked shut.

"Hey! Did you hear that?" said a male voice. An elf judging by the sound. It figured. Nobody's got sharper senses than a damned wood-elf. The cops are thick with them. Not only do wood-elves have heightened senses that would make a dire wolf jealous, but they have perfect gray skin, eyes that are violet or gold or crystal blue, and hair that Elvis would've killed for.

A FOOL THERE WAS

They are tall, sometimes more than five feet(!) and they all look like movie stars.

Bastards. I hate 'em all. What's the big deal about pretty eyes and a clear complexion anyway? That stuff's overrated. It's all physical. Show me a wood-elf with any business sense, and I'll eat my hat. They couldn't show a profit with a million dollars in t-bills. I made twenty grand last year just betting on penny stocks. No wonder I can't stand cops.

I crawled to my feet and went tiptoeing down the hallway before the coppers got wise to the secret door. I followed the passage to a stairwell, and followed it down. The stairs ended at a doorway. I checked the handle. It was unlocked, so I turned it slowly, pushing the door open just a crack. I peered out and saw a male centaur with glasses and a navy blue vest pushing a cart of office supplies down the hall. I waited for him to pass, and then stepped quietly out.

I heard the chime of the elevator doors around the corner and made a beeline in that direction. Naturally, just as I reached the corner, a whole herd of security goons came rushing out. I hurried back the way I had come. I tried to go back into the secret stairwell, but the door had automatically locked behind me. I saw a few more doorways up ahead, but they all led into busy offices. Then I saw the restrooms. I broke into a run.

A dwarf was coming out as I plowed through the door. He was four feet tall with a neatly trimmed beard, wearing a pinstriped business suit. I nearly slammed right into him. He looked me up and down as I pushed past him.

"Looks like you had the tuna salad, too," he joked. I smiled weakly and ducked into a booth.

I stood there a minute, trying to get my bearings. I had a long way to go before I was home free, and the building was crawling with security guards and cops, all of them looking for me. I considered trying to disguise myself and immediately dismissed the idea. There's no disguising the fact that you're a goblin.

On the other hand, I thought, I could ditch my trench coat and hat in the trash, and find a respectable jacket somewhere. That idea wasn't half-bad. I bet the cops wouldn't even look twice at a middle-aged goblin wearing a cardigan sweater. But where to get the disguise?

In one of the offices, I thought. Almost certainly, someone would have left a jacket or sweater on a coat hook, or hanging from the back of a chair. Piece of cake. I just had to find what I was looking for before anyone noticed me.

I was about to step out of the booth when I heard loud voices, and a burly hobgoblin security guard came bursting into the restroom. I stood there, quietly grimacing as he came my way. His heavy footsteps came closer, stopped as he paused to open each of the doors on the way down the line. I quietly slid the door lock into place.

At last, he reached my door. I saw thick, scaly green fingers reach over the top of the door. He gave it a hard yank, but the lock held firmly.

"Hey!" he bellowed in a deep, gravelly voice. "Who's in there?"

"Bug off," I said. "I'm trying to pinch a loaf in here, buddy!"

The hobgoblin chuckled. "Sorry," he said. "Watch out for that tuna salad." He checked the other booths and then left. I took a deep breath and sighed. That was a close call.

A FOOL THERE WAS

I gave the guard a minute to get out of sight, and then I put my plan into action. I took the ledger I'd swiped from Pretty Boy's safe out of my trench coat and placed it on the edge of the sink. I tossed my hat and coat in the trash, and then checked my face in the mirror. I wet my hands in the faucet and smeared my wild hair back into place.

Satisfied that I was at least half-presentable, I gathered up the ledger and then peeked out into the hallway. I saw a few office workers moving back and forth down the hall, but no security. I stepped out of the bathroom and headed for the elevators. I tried to look like I belonged there.

I slowed down to peer casually into each office as I strolled by. I was looking for a place that was quiet, a placed with cubicles, where no one would notice me moving around, taking things. Unfortunately, most of the offices were rather small and crowded. I didn't feel confident walking into a place like that, where everyone knew each other and no matter where I went, *someone* would always be watching. I stepped around the corner, and opportunity hit me like a boot in the face.

The centaur I had seen earlier was standing next to the elevator, leaning against the door to keep it from closing. He was talking to an attractive female elf with forest green hair. Just behind them, I saw the cart waiting inside the elevator. I could tell that the centaur was quite distracted. I hurried over and stepped around him to get inside. He glanced at me over his shoulder.

"This elevator's taken," he said dismissively. "Try the other one."

My hackles went up, partly because I knew that if I was a seven-foot hobgoblin he wouldn't have dared talk to me like that, and partly because I just hate centaurs. They've got egos almost as big as high-elves. I tried to keep my temper in check.

"I'm in a hurry," I said as politely as I could manage.

"Too bad."

My hand was already in my pocket, seeking out that big stainless steel ring, but I paused. The last thing I wanted to do was split the guy's skull open right there in front of the lady. Not that I was worried about frightening her; I just knew that the first thing she'd do would be to call security. In order to avoid that, I'd have to drag her along with me, which the cops tend to frown on. They always give it bad sounding names like "kidnapping," or "wrongful imprisonment." Drama, drama. Sometimes you just need to control a situation, that's all. I don't see why they have to make such a big deal out of everything.

At any rate, I didn't want to go through all that. So far, the cops didn't have much on me that they could make stick. Nothing that would ever hold up in court, anyway. I just had to be careful not to give them any charges that *would* stick. I tried to put on a sincere smile.

"Look, I'll send your cart right back up," I said helpfully. I reached out and tapped the button for the first floor. The centaur glanced at the pretty elf and then back at me. I could see him weighing his options. He considered me an obnoxious distraction, but otherwise harmless.

Sure, he could beat the hell out of me if he wanted to, but if he resorted to violence, he'd probably lose the girl. Likewise, if I continued to pester him, she would tire of the distraction and leave. The only choice he really had was whether or not to continue his pursuit of the female in favor of me. Putting it like that, it didn't seem like much of a choice...

A FOOL THERE WAS

"Whatever," he said, waving me off.

I grinned as he returned his full attention to the young woman. The door slid shut. During the trip down, I snooped around the cart for anything useful. I found a pair of dorky-looking reading glasses and a pocket protector. I used 'em both. I had hoped for a jacket or sweater, something to alter my overall appearance, but I was going to have to make do with what I had. I donned my goofy makeshift disguise and then grabbed the cart by the handles.

The doors opened on the main floor of Pixieland's shopping mall, directly across from an exit. I pushed the cart out into the aisle and began weaving my way through the crowd. It didn't take long to notice the three cops standing at the front doors, handing out flyers with my picture on them. I glanced at one of the flyers in a satyr's hands as he walked by, and saw the snapshot of myself walking into the building an hour earlier. They'd pulled it from a security cam. It showed me wearing my coat and hat. Most people would never look for anything more.

Score one for me, I thought.

I turned aside and maneuvered the cart past the entrance, towards the Pink Pixie Pretzel stand, where I veered off to the side. I paused there, next to a mailbox. I grabbed a pre-stamped envelope from the cart and wrote my own address on the cover. Then I jammed the ledger inside and slid it into the mailbox. I instantly felt safer, knowing I wouldn't have to worry about having that thing in my possession if the cops picked up my scent. If they did get hold of me, that one piece of evidence would be off in limbo somewhere, and they'd never be able to prove I had been in Pretty Boy's apartment.

I kept a wary eye on the guards for a few more minutes, hoping they'd move on to another entrance. When that didn't happen, I realized that I was going to need a plan. I had the advantage of being somewhat disguised, but that wasn't enough to get me through those doors. What I needed was a distraction. Fortunately, I'm excellent at improvising solutions to unexpected problems.

I took a minute to get everything sorted out just so. When I was ready, I gave the cart a good hard shove. I sent the cart full of reams of paper, files, and envelopes rolling straight towards the exit. Nobody even seemed to notice. It's not like a cart rolling around by itself is much of novelty in a mall full of fairies, elves, brownies, and dwarves.

About thirty feet from the exit, the cart burst into flames. That was my doing, of course. I hadn't done it long distance; my skill doesn't work that way. I had very carefully created a *small* fire in the bottom of the cart, specifically designed to take a few seconds before growing into a *big* fire. The flames came leaping out a little quicker than I'd hoped, but the overall effect still worked nicely. Several women screamed, and a flood of shoppers scattered out in every direction.

The cart rolled to a halt, billowing out a dark gray cloud that went rushing up towards the ceiling. I walked a few yards over to the nearest fire alarm and pulled the lever. The ear-splitting shriek filled the mall.

Predictably, the guards all came rushing to the rescue. Even from a distance, I could see how badly each and every one of them wanted to be a hero. They'd trained for an occasion such as this. They had worked and studied and prepared themselves for a chance to prove themselves worthy, to earn themselves a

A FOOL THERE WAS

moment of recognition that they would probably never equal if they lived a thousand years.

Morons.

Why is it that all the dumb saps in the world wanna be a hero? Sometimes it seems like every hero is a buffoon and every bad guy is an evil genius. I suppose that's because it takes a genius to know where the real money is, and that it usually involves some sort of crime. I shouldn't complain that all the good guys are imbeciles. It just makes my job that much easier.

I slipped around the corner, right behind the distracted guards, and walked straight out the front doors. The sprinklers came on behind me. I casually strolled down the long row of concrete stairs, breathing in deeply of the undercity air. It smelled like diesel fumes, mildew, and cotton candy. Pure heaven.

I glanced up towards the big black roof of the cavern and saw the multicolored lights of a million pixies blinking and zooming erratically back and forth through the wispy clouds. I saw the lights of the city stretching out in every direction, a million strangers all doing their own things all at once. I smiled. It was good to be free again.

A red and yellow cable car waited at the street, and I could see the driver getting ready to take off. I hurried over. As I climbed the steps, I took off the centaur's reading glasses and tossed them under the wheels. I dropped a gold penny into the machine and took a seat. As we pulled away from the curb, I glanced up towards the mall entrance and saw the guards inside, continuing their valiant struggle to get the burning cart under control. Someone produced a fire extinguisher. It didn't put out the fire, but it made one hell of a dust cloud. The white powder slowly filled the entrance, pushing up against the windows until they went white and everything inside disappeared.

I grinned and leaned back in my seat. All things considered, I was proud of how well I'd managed things. Despite being set up for a murder and being seen by dozens of witnesses, I'd managed to get out of the place intact. Sure, the cops were after me, but I knew for a fact that they didn't have anything on me. My presence in the mall wasn't enough to convict me of anything, and nobody had even seen me in Pretty Boy's flat. I'd been very careful not to leave any evidence behind. I was free as a bird. Plus, I'd have a very nice package coming in the mail soon; something I could use to blackmail, bribe, and extort for years to come...

It was the setup that bothered me. I was already convinced that was exactly what it was. There's no such thing as a coincidence, especially when it comes to a situation like this. Honey Love had sent me into that building on the exact same night that Pretty Boy happened to be murdered. No, I wasn't buying that. Honey had set me up. Now I just had to find her and wring her scrawny little neck until she confessed.

A thin smile came to my lips. I couldn't wait to see the look on Honey's face when she found out I was not only still alive, but I hadn't even been arrested! It was going to be one for the books. I checked my watch, and noted that she'd probably still be at work. That was, if she had bothered going to work at all. After stealing that diamond, she was probably on her way to Paris or the Mediterranean. I decided to stop by her dressing room just in case.

A FOOL THERE WAS

Right in the middle of my thoughts, a big green hand with fingers the size of German sausages clamped down on my shoulder. I almost crapped my pants. I was sure one of those hobgoblin security goons had caught up to me.

I turned slowly, my heart hammering in my chest, right hand digging into my pocket in search of my power ring... and gazed up into the fiery dark green eyes of my mortal enemy, the Steward: *Hank Mossberg!*

Chapter 5

"What are you up to, Sam?" Mossberg said in a voice like a truck full of gravel bouncing down the highway. He was wearing his fedora hat and an old brown trench coat, like always. He looked like a bigger, uglier version of me. And poorer, of course. I wanted to ask him if he'd been shopping at Goodwill, but decided against it. I licked my lips nervously.

Hank Mossberg is the Steward. What does that mean? Well, it's sort of like a sheriff. See, in the old days, ogres were the lawmen of the fae. They kept the peace between the different races of fairy creatures, and protected them from humans. One reason this task fell to the ogres is that they're bigger than just about anybody else. In the old days, some of them were over twenty feet tall. Hank's just a little ogre, but he's still close to seven feet, and probably two hundred and forty pounds.

Another reason is that magic doesn't work on ogres. They're like lightning rods. In fact, even though Mossberg wasn't touching my skin, I could already feel a slow drain on my energy, working right through my shirt and into his hand. I twisted awkwardly away before the stupid oaf knocked me unconscious.

"Just doing a little window shopping," I said cleverly.

Hank raised an eyebrow. "Shopping, huh? Should I check your pockets?"

"Very funny. Is that any way to talk to an old friend?"

"No, but it'll work for you."

Hank glanced back at the mall, but thankfully the cable car had pulled away from the curb and he couldn't see what was going on inside from that distance. I knew from the look on his face that he was completely unaware of all that had transpired. See what I mean about cops? Dumb as rocks.

"Haven't seen you around lately," Hank grumbled. "It was nice."

"I keep myself busy. Some of us gotta work for a living."

He made a grumbling sound.

"Where's that partner of yours?" I said. "The dwarf? What's his name, Butch or something like that?"

Hank leaned back in his seat and fixed his gaze on some distant point. "Retired," he said. "Married. He's got a baby now."

"Too bad," I mumbled. "He was a great poker player. I guess that's why he hasn't been around *The Drunken Unicorn* lately."

An awkward silence fell over us. I heard the low voices of the other passengers, the sounds of traffic, the creaking of the cable car's chassis. I was growing more uncomfortable with every passing second. I didn't like the idea that while Hank was staring off into space, he might be *thinking* about something. I decided it was best to keep him distracted. I said something.

"So you working on a case?"

"None of your business."

"Aww, come on. Just 'cause we're competitors doesn't mean we can't talk shop."

"We are *not* competitors. I'm the Steward. You're a scumbag."

A FOOL THERE WAS

"Stop, you're making me blush."

Hank leaned forward, bracing his massive elbows on the back of the seat. He pushed the brim of his hat back so he could glare at me. I felt the seat frame bending under his weight.

"I don't know what you're up to, Snyvvle," he said in a half-whisper that resembled the low-throated rumble of a lion's growl. "But I'm watching you. You remember that, goblin."

I grinned nervously, and the hairs rose all over my body. Hank's an apex predator, there's no doubt about that. That voice of his could make Mother Goose sound like Stephen King.

"I'm offended," I said quickly. "You don't trust me, Hank?"

"I don't trust anyone, especially you."

Maybe you're not as dumb as I thought... "I see my stop coming up. It was nice talking to you."

"Keep your nose clean. And remember what I said."

I jumped out of my seat and hurried down the steps, trying not to appear nervous even though I was crawling out of my skin. I touched down lightly on the sidewalk and started hoofing it up the street towards *Fairyblooms*. I forced myself not to look back until I heard the sound of the cable car pulling away. Then I braved a glance over my shoulder. Hank was nowhere to be seen. He was gone.

I took a deep breath, and tried to stop my knees from knocking together. That was a close call. I needed to start paying more attention to my surroundings. Hank hadn't heard about my misadventures in *Pixieland*, but if he had, things would have turned out very differently. He'd had the jump on me, and one touch from him could have knocked me out cold. Instead of walking around downtown, I'd have been sleeping it off in his dingy little jail cell under the Mother tree awaiting my murder trial.

Hank's jail is located down in the roots under the Mother tree. The Mother is a massive tree about twenty stories tall. She's located topside, in northern San Francisco, west of the Financial District. She is one of the oldest living creatures on earth, and she carries the seed for every kind of tree known to man. The Mother and her kind existed long before humans came along, and even before the fae, and they'll probably be here long after we're all gone.

Personally, I can't figure out why the universe chose to make a plant capable of outliving everything else on earth. It just doesn't make sense. Goblins are obviously far superior to all the other races, and our life-spans are a mere two hundred years at best. Life just isn't fair.

Still, with a quick wit and some decent business skills, even the lowliest goblin can do well for himself. I guess Mother Nature just feared that given enough time, goblins would become too great and powerful. She made sure we wouldn't live long enough to take over the whole universe.

A cold breeze blew down the back of my neck, and I grimaced. I needed another coat. You would think that with the undercity being located inside a gigantic cavern, there wouldn't be any such thing as weather. You'd be wrong. It gets cold and windy here, it gets foggy, sometimes it even clouds up and rains. Thankfully, the only thing that doesn't happen here is heat. It never gets hot in the undercity, because we're too deep in the earth, and because part of the cavern actually lies beneath the Pacific and the San Francisco Bay. Don't think that means it's not humid, though. Moss and mushrooms grow

A FOOL THERE WAS

everywhere down here. Even on your vehicle, if you let it sit still too long.

I was ready to call it a day, but I needed to pick up my car first. *Fairyblooms* was only two blocks away, so I decided to pick up a new coat and hat on the way to the parking garage. I hurried up the street, doing my best to ignore the chill in the air that was sending shivers down my spine. There were a few people on the streets, but being the middle of the night, most honest folks were at work.

Aside from being nocturnal, the undercity is just like any other city in that fashion. We have rush hours, holidays, the whole nine yards. Technically though, we're not completely nocturnal anymore. Many of the fae and most of the kindred also do business topside, which means they need to be able to do their banking and such during the day, when humans are awake. Personally, I try to stick as close to my natural schedule as I can. I don't care for being awake during the day. It's unnatural.

When I walked into *Fairyblooms,* I immediately caught the eye of a manager. Retailers have a love-hate relationship with my kind. Goblin shoplifting skills are infamous, and we're notorious for trying to haggle deals out of the sales people. On the other hand, we *always* have money, and we tend to be attracted to shiny things like jewelry. That means a good salesperson can actually make a lot of money off us, if he's smart. Assuming of course, that he can manage to keep us from stealing half the store out from under his nose at the same time.

I could tell the manager was watching me from the moment I walked through the doors. I confirmed this as I took the escalator up to the men's department. I stepped around the corner, out of sight, and she promptly appeared behind me. I leapt out and surprised her.

"Boo!" I said. I caught her by the arm and she shrieked.

"Easy, honey," I said with a wink. "Just testing your observational skills."

"Get away from me," she said, yanking her arm back. I could tell from the pouty look on her face that she was embarrassed. It was cute. She was tall, part human and part something else, I couldn't be sure what. But she had dark hair and big blue eyes and a set of curves that would make the Autobahn jealous. The nametag on her shirt read **Ruby,** and in smaller lettering underneath: MANAGER.

"Let me make it up to you, Ruby," I said. "I need a new coat. If you sell it to me personally, I'll pay full price. I'll even throw in a tip."

She blinked her long dark lashes at me, and bit her lower lip. Sexy. If she kept it up, she might sell me a lot more than a coat. "All right," she said at last. "Only if you promise not to steal anything."

"You're breaking my heart, dollface. Do I look like some urchin off the street?"

She looked me up and down, and frowned. I glanced down at my clothes and suddenly remembered all that I'd just been through. I instantly regretted pointing out my appearance.

"Never mind that," I said, taking her by the arm. "Looks like I might need a new shirt, too." I reached into my pocket and withdrew a wad of bills. Human money. They like that down here just as well as anything. "How's that?" I said, flashing my roll of green. Her eyes brightened and a smile crept over her features.

A FOOL THERE WAS

"Right this way, sir."

It didn't take long for Ruby to set me up with a nice tweed coat and a classy felt hat. I also bought three shirts and tried on a few rings, but didn't buy any. I did slip one into my pocket, just for kicks. When she walked me to the doors, I thanked her for everything and swatted her on the ass.

"Hey, watch it!" she said. "Don't make me call security."

"Just testing the waters, dollface."

What she didn't know was that while swatting her, I returned the ring. I slipped it into the small pocket in her skirt, along with my business card. I left after that, grinning from ear to ear. Now it was just a matter of waiting to see what she'd do. When would she find the ring? While she was at work, or later, possibly at home? When she found it, would she return it, or keep it for herself? Either way, I had won, because I knew she'd never forget what had happened. And some day, when she needed something, she'd come calling. Eventually, they all come calling...

After leaving the department store, I hurried up the street to the parking garage. The elevator was broken, so I took the stairs up to the third floor where I'd parked. The concrete stairwell was slippery with moss and condensation, so I walked slowly. As I reached the top, I heard voices nearby:

"What time is it?" said a gruff voice, maybe a goblin.

"Ummm. Four a.m." That was a hobgoblin. The bigger they get, the dumber they are. His voice sounded like a braying moose. "Where is he, Boss?"

"How should I know? All I know is we're waiting here 'till he comes back."

JAMIE SEDGWICK

My shoulders slumped. I took another step up and peeked through the railing, across the floor of the garage. It was just as I'd figured: a goblin and a hobgoblin. The two mobsters dressed in black suits waited impatiently near my car. Their intentions were fairly clear. Moose paced back and forth, pausing now and then to lean on the stock of his tommy gun. The goblin leaned back against the railing, openly displaying two Colt .45's dangling from shoulder holsters. The holsters were brightly colored, as if they were made out of Skittles. I was skeptical about whether the goblin could actually wield those weapons without hurting himself, but it was best not to find out.

I pursed my lips. The smartest thing to do at this point would have been to take a walk. I was outnumbered and outgunned. Even without the weapons, that hobgoblin could have ripped my limbs off one by one. Problem though, is that I take my car very seriously. It's the only one like it in the undercity, and one of very few left topside. It also has a certain sentimental value, because it's the first car I ever bought. That was back in my lean days, when I was stealing and hustling just to keep a full belly.

I was also working two full-time jobs, one as a line cook at the very restaurant I'd been stealing from for all those years, the other as a bicycle messenger. Goblins aren't averse to hard work, as long as there's a paycheck in it. I've never worked more than four jobs at once, though. If you take it too far the work suffers, followed immediately by the paycheck. It's what I call diminishing returns.

I bought that hot rod after my first legitimate detective job. It all started one night while hanging out at the *Drunken*

A FOOL THERE WAS

Unicorn. I happened to cross paths with a bounty hunter. Her name was Belle, and she was an attractive kindred with gnomish, elven, and human ancestors. She was tracking a half-troll who was wanted topside for jumping bail. After a few games of pool and quite a few shots of whisky, I decided to give Belle a hand. She wasn't from the area, so she didn't know the city the way I did.

Turned out the suspect had started a ring of car thieves, and had imported a bunch of rare automobiles to sell to rich collectors in the undercity. I led Belle to her bail jumper, and in the process closed a major case for the undercity cops. The chief of police gave me a healthy reward, which I used to buy the '29 Ford they had impounded before it went to auction. The rest of the cops never forgave me. They had been planning on snatching it up for themselves.

I didn't care. I saw that car and wanted it. I didn't owe those chumps anything. Besides, if they'd been busy catching the car thieves instead of hanging out at donut shops and trying to look busy while circling endlessly in their cruisers, they would have closed that case instead of me.

Tough cookies. That's what I told 'em, and still do, every chance I get.

After buying my car, I had enough money left to rent an apartment and get myself licensed. With my name all over the papers, I knew I'd never get a better opportunity to go into business. That's exactly what I did. I capitalized on that fame to rake in the profits with my detective business for several years.

That was, until Hank Mossberg showed up and took the spotlight. Suddenly everyone started going to him with their problems. After all, he's such a nice guy, and he works for *free*. What a dumbass.

So now you understand why leaving my car in the hands of those two goons was unacceptable. I crept along the back wall, ducking behind the row of automobiles. I worked my way around the back of the garage and then back towards my car from behind. Hovering in the shadows, I closed in from the far side, ducking out of sight as the occasional vehicle went driving by.

I crept up behind the passenger side of my car, opposite the two thugs, and ducked down under the wheel well. Very quietly, I hung my new shirts from the door handle.

I waited there until I felt Moose leaning up against my car. His weight moved the whole vehicle. He sighed loudly.

"Get up, you lazy mook," the goblin said.

"I'm tired," Moose replied in a whiny voice.

"If you don't get on your feet, I'll pump you so full of lead the coroner will think you're a block of swiss cheese."

They were distracted, so I pounced. "Hey, Moose!" I shouted. I leapt out from behind the car and took a swing at the hobgoblin with my enchanted ring. He saw me and went fumbling for his tommy gun, but I was already on top of him. Figuratively speaking, of course, since he was more than twice my height.

I hammered him a good solid shot in the gut. He blew out a gust of hot air and doubled over. I took a step back and let him drop to his knees in front of me. The goblin tossed his cigarette aside and went for his .45's, but he wasn't fast enough. I had my taser out in a flash. I aimed it square at his chest and fired. Unfortunately, I didn't take into account that we were a

A FOOL THERE WAS

good four yards apart. The taser's two probes shot out of the gun in an arcing trajectory that lost altitude quick. I ended up hitting him somewhat below the mark. Or rather, *below the belt,* as they say in boxing.

The probes hit home and the goblin screamed loud enough to rattle my eardrums. He flopped to the ground like a fairy with its wings pulled off. He was doubled over, moaning and shaking on the concrete, both hands pressed into his crotch.

I turned my attention back to the hobgoblin, who was still on his knees. I raised my fist to nail him on the chin.

"Don't!" Moose cried out, waving his arms in the air. "Don't hurt me anymore."

"I'm gonna hurt ya, bub," I said. "That is, unless you tell me what you and your pal there were doing with my car."

"We didn't do nuthin'!" he cried out. "We were just waitin' for ya, that's all."

"Uh-huh. Waiting to put the squeeze on good old Sammy, eh? What were you gonna do, break my legs? Fill me up with hot lead?"

"It's your own fault!" the goblin wheezed. He was still on the ground with his hands clutched between his legs and two probes sticking out of his wanger, or close enough to it to make me cringe.

"Come again?" I said. "How's it my fault?"

"You killed Pretty Boy," said Moose.

"And you stole his diamond."

I should have known it was only a matter of time before the rest of Pretty Boy's crew came gunning for me. I honestly couldn't blame them. They had no way of knowing I didn't kill their boss. They had just as much reason to suspect me as the cops. More, actually, because the gang probably knew about the missing ledger, and that was one thing I *actually had* stolen.

"You're wrong, boys," I said quickly. "I was hired to look into that diamond. I'll admit that much. But I didn't take it."

I snatched the tommy gun off the ground. I opened the door to my car and tossed it on the back seat. Then I relieved the goblin of his pistols and tossed them in back as well. I grabbed my shirts and settled in behind the wheel. I slammed the door shut, rolled the window down, and stuck my head out.

"When I got to Pretty Boy's place, that rock was gone and he was dead. That's the long and short of it, and that's more than I should have told you already. So stay off my back!"

"It doesn't matter," the goblin said venomously. "Pretty Boy's brother will be in town tomorrow night. When he gets here, it's all over for you, Snyvvle."

"Sure it is," I said, starting up the engine. I put the car in reverse and backed out of the parking spot.

"You're dead!" the goblin shouted after me. "You've got twenty-four hours, Snyvvle. You hear me? Twenty-four hours and you're dead!"

I didn't bother to respond. I was in a hurry. I had a date with an angel. An angel named Honey who was about to get her wings ripped off. I slammed it into gear and lit up the tires, leaving my two attackers choking on a cloud of rubbery black smoke.

Chapter 6

Honey worked at a joint called *The Lounge,* a nightclub located in the northeastern corner of the Downtown district. It's one of a kind. It's huge, and it's the only building in all the undercity that connects directly with the topside. Up in San Francisco, *The Lounge* looks like just another building. It's a nightclub up there, too. What the humans don't know is that the building has roots that go all the way down, right into Baliztra. I can only imagine what a human might think, if in a drunken stupor he somehow managed to take the elevator all the way down and stumbled out into the undercity.

I had to laugh at the idea. A drunken human walking around Baliztra, gawking at all the fairies and elves and unicorns. The idea was so funny that I made up my mind on the spot to do it. In seconds, I had planned the whole thing out: I would take the stairs up to one of the clubs and lurk in the shadows until I had attracted the attention of some over credulous mortal. I would lure him back down into the darkness, down the many long flights of stairs, right into the heart of the undercity. I would stay just out of reach, just beyond the next corner, taunting him forward, one step at a time, until finally it was too late.

Then, as the drunk stumbled out into the street, his gaze tracking back and forth wildly in disbelief, I would rush out of the darkness and start screaming and baring my fangs. If that didn't kill him on the spot, I would sing and dance around him like a fool while he fell to his knees and begged me to spare his miserable mortal life.

Then, of course, the Elders would show up. Sooner or later, someone always calls the Elders. After their arrival, the next thing my victim knew, he would be waking up in a park somewhere topside with a foggy head and no memory of the previous night.

I sighed. *Elders*. Damn do-gooders ruin everything. What's the point in going to all the work of such an extravagant prank when the Elders can come along and erase a mortal's memory with a snap of their fingers? They just take the fun out of everything. They really take the wind out of my sails. No wonder the undercity's no fun anymore.

It didn't take long to get back across town. When I got there, I found I had just missed a storm. Bourbon Street was rain-slicked and glistening, the neon lights of the bars and clubs reflected in mirror-like pools on the asphalt. I parked across the street from *The Lounge* and sat in the car a minute, scoping out the scene. I wanted to make sure the coppers hadn't gotten there first.

When I was sure it was all clear, I hurried across the street and stepped into the lobby. The place was dimly lit and smoky, like always. The first thing I noticed was the smell of whisky and cigar smoke, followed by the faint acid aroma of illegal pixie dust. The sounds of music came rolling out; the steady rhythm of hooves and feet stamping to the beat, the cheers and laughter of a well-entertained crowd. I smiled. *The Lounge* is my kind of place.

A FOOL THERE WAS

The two bouncers in the back took little note of me as I wandered in. The place was packed, and I glanced over the crowd towards the stage. Actually, there are three stages, the outer ones connected by long narrow catwalks to the main stage at the back of the room. This allows for an excellent view no matter where you happen to be seated. That's one reason *The Lounge* is always full. Another reason is that drinks are always half-price for the ladies. They even have a ladies' night twice a week, where male satyrs and hobgoblins do stripteases and the women get to enjoy the show. Yeah, real classy. Politically correct, even.

I ignored the small stages. The girls dancing there were pretty, but they weren't the focus of my attention. Honey was, and she was on the main stage. To be honest, I was a bit surprised she was there. Now that she had her diamond, the smart thing to do would have been to skip town. Maybe she was just keeping up appearances until she made all her arrangements. Or maybe something else was keeping her there; something I hadn't thought of.

Honey's long red dress was gone now. The classy lounge singer part of her act was over. She had stripped down to a bikini top and g-string and she was doing a dance that almost made me forget who I was and why I was there. I caught myself falling under her spell and yanked my gaze away. I took a deep breath. That was close.

I circled around the main stage and stepped behind the curtain. I found a big, nasty-looking hobgoblin waiting for me. He had a long green goatee, so dark that it was black in the dim lighting of the club, and a bone piercing through the ridge of his nose. He had tribal art tattoos that covered the left side of his face and most of his shaved head. He was wearing trousers, the loose fitting kind that martial artists like to wear, and no shirt. His nipples were pierced too, with large silver hoops.

"No guests," he said in a voice like gears grinding in a semi-truck. I flashed him my detective badge.

"I'm here on business," I said.

"No guests," he repeated, and then glanced over my head as if to dismiss me.

I was torn. Part of me wanted to reach up and grab those nipple rings and swing from them like a gymnast. I wanted to give him a good hard lesson in common sense, and the mere thought brought a wicked grin to my face. Unfortunately, the other part of me knew that if I did something like that, any chance I'd had of talking to Honey would go right out the door. In fact, they'd probably never let me into *The Lounge* again. As much as it would have pleased me to rip off that bouncer's nipples and parade around the stage with them, it was certainly not in my best interest.

"You like magic?" I said.

"What?"

"Magic tricks? You like 'em?"

"Beat it, buddy, before I beat you."

"Check your pocket."

"Huh?" Finally, he lowered his gaze to look at me.

"Your front pocket. Check it."

He rolled his eyes and shook his head, but couldn't resist the temptation. He reached into his trousers and pulled out a fifty. His eyes widened, and he looked at me.

"How'd you do that?"

A FOOL THERE WAS

"I don't know what you're talking about," I said with a grin. "Check your other pocket."

He did, and pulled out another fifty. He held them both up, smiling from ear to ear. "You're pretty good," he said.

"Thanks. So how about it? You think I could take a peek at that dressing room?"

He peeked out through the curtain. He looked around, checking to see that nobody had been watching us. "All right," he said. "Ten minutes." He shoved the bills back into his pocket and stood aside.

"Thank you, kind sir," I said, brushing past him.

I hurried down the hall and turned the corner. Then I reached into my pocket and pulled out the two fifties I'd just stolen back from him. I smiled as I slid them back into my money roll. The guard was a hobgoblin, so I was pretty sure he was too dumb to realize that whatever I had put into his pockets, I could take out as well. He should just be glad I didn't take his wallet, too.

That thought was enough to stop me in my tracks. *Why hadn't I taken his wallet?* It's not like me to pass up such an easy mark, especially one with a lousy attitude. *Business,* I told myself. *It's bad for business.*

I satisfied myself with that answer, but deep down inside I couldn't help worrying that I might be losing my edge. Maybe the easy life was taking a toll on me. Maybe the booze, the cigars, and legitimate work were all working against me, turning me into something I shouldn't be. That was bad. Goblins are a Darwinian species if there ever was one. It's all about survival of the fittest. When a goblin lets himself get weak and lazy, he's just begging to have his throat cut.

I continued down the hall with a stern reminder echoing in the back of my head: *Stay sharp. Don't be a sucker.* Then I came to Honey's room. Her name was on the door, and it was unlocked. I stepped inside and waited.

It took a while for Honey to finish her show. I wasn't worried about the guard coming after me, because hobgoblins don't have the mental capacity to remember something that happened more than five minutes ago. He had probably already forgotten about me, and about the hundred bucks, too.

Honey came into the room with her dress and bikini top draped over her arm. She was still wearing the g-string and heels, but that was all. She couldn't see me because I had positioned myself behind a costume rack, next to the closet. I was sitting in a folding chair, little more than a thin shadow in the darkness behind her.

Honey was in good form, her pale translucent skin glistened with sweat, strands of long blonde hair clinging to her back and shoulders. Part of me just wanted to sit there and watch her for a while. Another part wanted to reach out and strangle her. She settled down in front of the mirror and started wiping the sweat from her face with a towel.

"Too bad you don't have a shower in here," I said.

She made a jerking movement and then raised her gaze to stare at my reflection in the mirror.

"I wasn't expecting you," she said. "Are you done already?"

I rose out of the chair and walked up behind her, staring back at her gorgeous, glistening reflection. "I had a little trouble," I said, narrowing my eyes.

Her face hardened. "Don't tell me you lost it?"

A FOOL THERE WAS

I felt the muscles tense up all over my body. I can usually tell when somebody's jerking me around, but if she was lying, I couldn't see it. I looked at her closely and what I saw written all over her face was worry. *Did I lose the diamond? Did Pretty Boy find out what she was up to?* I decided to give her a little test.

"I had a talk with Pretty Boy," I said.

She went tense. Very slowly, she set the towel on the bench and turned to face me. When she spoke, her voice was tight as a rubber band about to snap. It cracked nervously as she said, "What happened?"

"You lied to me."

Her eyes widened. I could practically see her heart hammering inside her chest. She took a deep breath, drawing my attention to the fact that she was still almost entirely nude and just as stunning as the Alps in winter. I clenched my jaw, forcing myself to keep eye contact. She lowered her gaze.

"I'm sorry. I thought that if you knew..."

"Knew what?" I said with a snarl. "Come on, out with it! I know what you're up to!"

"About me and Pretty Boy. About the diamond. Maybe it was never mine Sam, but it *should have* been. Don't you see that? After all the hurt, all the hard things he did to me? Don't you see that I deserved it?"

"I see that you set me up," I said, putting my hands on the armrests and leaning in so that my long, crooked nose was an inch from hers. "Was that your plan? To steal the diamond and have me take the fall? Or was I supposed to get killed?"

Her gaze snapped back to me. She frowned, and her eyebrows formed perfect curling lines across her brow that damn near melted my cold goblin heart. *Why women? Why must I have this weakness?*

"I don't know what you mean," she said breathlessly. "Nothing was supposed to happen to you, Sam."

I raised the back of my hand, and she flinched.

"Please, Sam. Don't hurt me. I don't want anyone to hurt me anymore."

I lowered my hand and turned away, frustrated. I could tell she really meant it. Pretty Boy hadn't been good to her. That was why she'd hired me to steal the diamond. It was for revenge.

"Why didn't you tell me the truth from the start?"

"I couldn't. I knew you'd need a good reason to get involved. I had to make up that story about Pretty Boy stealing the diamond."

She didn't know me very well. All she'd really had to do was tell me about the diamond. It was almost worth all the trouble. Then again, so was she.

"Well if you didn't set me up, then who?" I said angrily. "Who else is in on this?"

"Please, Sam, I don't know what you mean. There is nobody else."

She rose from her chair and stepped around behind me. Her arms snaked in around my chest and I felt the firmness of her breasts against my back. Honey stood a good eighteen inches taller than me, which made it easy for her sweet, hot breath to raise the hairs on the back of my neck. My body shuddered at her touch, and all my thoughts flew south for the winter. Suddenly it was just me and her, all alone in that cold, dark dressing room.

A FOOL THERE WAS

"Sam, tell me what happened," she begged. "Please."

"Why?" I snapped. "So you can go running back to Pretty Boy and apologize for everything that happened? So you can point the finger at me and make good and sure I end up with a broken neck?"

"Never," she whispered into my ear, sending chills crawling up and down my entire body. "I could never go back to him, Sam. Can't you see that I'm terrified of him?"

I turned to face her. Honey relaxed her grip and rested her arms on my shoulders as I stared up into her face. I could see that she was telling the truth. Either that, or she was such a good liar that even I couldn't tell. Then again, with my face inches away from her gorgeous breasts, I couldn't be sure of anything. It took all I had just to keep the conversation going.

"I can't go back to him," she continued. "If I do, I'm afraid he'll kill me. He's not nice, Sam. He hurts people. Even the people he loves. He's a cruel, cruel man."

"Why were you with him?"

"I thought I loved him."

"And when he was beating on you, you thought he loved you then?"

She straightened her shoulders. "I took it," she said proudly. "I took it like a woman."

"A woman or a punching bag?"

"It doesn't make any difference now. It's all over. He's hurting others, now."

"Not anymore, he's not," I mumbled. She took a step back and stared down into my face.

"What do you mean?"

I gazed up at her, watching her reaction closely.

"Pretty Boy is dead."

I saw shock, concern, confusion. Honey was wondering what it all meant for her. If Pretty Boy was dead, she didn't have to worry about him anymore. But what about the diamond? If I'd killed him, I must have the diamond...

"Sam?"

"Honey."

"What happened?"

I looked her up and down, soaking it all in, hardly believing the words about to come out of my mouth:

"Put some clothes on," I said. "We'll get a bite to eat, and I'll tell you all about it."

I took Honey to a café not far from *The Lounge,* a quiet little barbecue joint called *The Golden Bison.* It has always been one of my favorite diners because it's the kind of place where you can enjoy a plate of ribs and a mug of beer in peace. The guy who runs the *Bison* -a dark dwarf who goes by the name Church- doesn't care who eats there as long as they pay. And he knows how to keep his mouth shut. He's a real class act.

I knew I wouldn't run into any coppers at the *Bison*, and probably nobody on Pretty Boy's payroll either. If I did run into some of Pretty Boy's goons, I knew Church would clean up the mess discreetly. The last thing he would want was a bunch of cops snooping around, asking questions.

Honey and I settled into a booth and a teenage female troll took our order. She wasn't much to look at, but her personality was lousy. I ordered for both of us: a platter of ribs with beer-battered fries, a cold lager for me and a red wine for Honey. Being a dryad, I expected her to put up a fight. Most dryads are vegetarians. To my surprise, Honey not only put

A FOOL THERE WAS

away more than her share of the ribs, she also dismissed the wine after two sips and ordered a pint of ale for herself. I glanced up at one point and saw her chin covered in barbecue sauce. I instantly fell head over heels in love. Suddenly I didn't care if this woman set me up for murder or pulled the trigger herself. If the bullet came from her, I'd love it just for that.

"What are you staring at?" she said, with a grin.

"Just thinking I'd better order some more food before you start eating the silverware."

"What's the matter? Am I not proper enough for you?"

"Not at all. I'm just worried if you keep eating like that, your ass will get as big as a house."

"You didn't seem to mind the way it looked earlier," she said with a wink. I instantly remembered the way it had looked, and I think I began to blush. Which for a greenskin doesn't mean much, except that my ears start to burn and I look uncomfortably warm. Honey reached over and tickled my chin.

"You're cute when you're embarrassed," she said.

"I'm not embarrassed," I said. "Just trying to figure out if I should kiss you or kill you."

"Let me help you with that." She leaned across the table, twisting her head to avoid my nose, and planted a long, wet, barbecue-flavored kiss on my lips. I forgot pretty much everything else.

A few moments after she pulled away, I realized that I had been staring at her and I wasn't sure how long. I blinked, swooning like a schoolboy, and she smiled at me. Dryads have that effect on men. Women in general have that effect on goblins.

"Does that help you make up your mind?" she said, which didn't make much sense because I couldn't hardly remember anything we'd just said. I played it cool and took a long swig of my beer, still tasting the sweetness of her mouth on my lips.

"Don't be like that," she said in a pouty voice. "I can't take the silent treatment, Sam. Don't you trust me now?"

"Sure, I trust you," I said, bringing it all back into focus.

"Then won't you tell me what happened with Dave?"

I sighed. I leaned back in my chair and told her the whole story... leaving out a few minor details of course, like the ledger I'd lifted out of his safe. When I was finished, Honey didn't know what to think.

"It wasn't me," she insisted. "I don't know who killed him, or how they knew about the diamond, but it wasn't me."

"Then who?" I said. "Who else could have known?"

"I don't know... maybe somebody in his gang. Pretty Boy was connected with lots of unsavory sorts."

"Such as?"

"Who do you think? Criminals, thieves, killers."

"There has to be somebody," I said. "Someone he trusted maybe, or someone who was close enough to know about the diamond, and how to get it."

"You mean besides me?" she said. "Okay, sure. Maybe Pretty Boy had other girls. I don't know. I didn't pry into his affairs of *any* kind."

"Meaning?"

"Oh, come now," she said. "I know you've heard the rumors."

I stared at her, waiting for an explanation.

"About the hobgoblins."

A FOOL THERE WAS

I raised my eyebrows. She rolled her eyes.

"Look, I don't know if it's true or not, but there were rumors going around that Pretty Boy had a thing for young hobgoblins."

"Males?" I said in disbelief.

"Have you ever seen a female hobgoblin?"

"Come to think of it, no I haven't."

"That's because they don't exist. Hobgoblins are a hybrid species that can't produce females. Only males. No matter who they mate with, the offspring is always a male hobgoblin, and it's always a pureblood."

"How's that that possible?" I said. "Genetics don't work like that."

She rolled her eyes again. "I thought you were smarter than that, Sam. We're talking about the fae. Since when the do the principles of human science apply to fairy creatures?"

My head was spinning, and not because of the hobgoblin thing. It was because Honey had suddenly turned out to be a lot smarter than I'd pegged her for. The realization was enough to remind me to stay on my toes. It didn't matter how much I loved her, or lusted for her, or wanted to die for just one more kiss... The fact was that I still didn't know if she could be trusted. And now she'd slipped up and let me see that she was smart. That almost certainly meant I *could not* trust her.

I glanced at my watch. "I think it's time for me to be going," I said. Honey looked worried.

"Just like that? You're going to leave me all alone?"

"You'll be fine," I promised. I meant it, too. Even if the goons did come looking for her, I knew she could outsmart them the way she'd outsmarted me. Honey had it all going for her. Not just looks, but street smarts, too. She was a dangerous package. No, I wasn't worried about her at all.

I took Honey out front and hailed her a cab. By then, traffic was starting to pick up for the morning commute, which is by far the worst traffic of the day. Thousands of fae creatures going home for the day, others going to work, others taking kids to school and going shopping. It's the stuff of nightmares, truly. Especially since there's not one single road or highway in the undercity that's got more than two lanes.

Thankfully, it didn't take long to get onto the highway. From there, it was a short loop to the south end of the lake. By the time I got back to the Hallows, things were once again quiet and foggy. I parked out front like usual, and glanced at the upstairs window in my office. The curtains were partially drawn and I saw the dim shadowy shape of my coat rack near the opposite door. Everything looked just as I'd left it.

I climbed the stairs out front and reached for the brass door handle, but froze with my hand on the knob. Down at the corner of the door, I saw the faintest traces of charred residue marring the wood. It was nothing more than a smudge, the only trace of a much larger mark that someone had purposefully wiped away.

I bristled. I knew instantly that someone had been inside my office. The charring was the sign of a protection spell that had been bypassed by an intruder. If the spell had gone off successfully, the intruder would have been blasted by a jolt of lightning that should have paralyzed him for half an hour. That would have given the cops time to get there, and for the second half of the spell to dial my cell phone and alert me to the situation. Since neither of those things had happened, I

A FOOL THERE WAS

could only assume whoever it was had managed to get inside successfully.

I had no way of knowing if the intruder was still inside, so I very quietly slipped down the alley and opened the hidden door to my basement. I felt around for the brick with the secret switch behind it, and then pressed it ever so gently. There was a *clicking* sound inside the wall, and the bricks separated neatly, making a jagged line as the door swung outward.

I installed that door myself. I purposefully did it without magic, because powerful mages like high-elves, Elders, and the Maji can all detect the presence of spells. The nice thing about being surrounded by so many powerful magic users is that they depend on their powers so often, they forget that some things can be done just as easily without magic. Because of that, they don't look for trap doors. They look for magic portals. They don't look for hidden locks, they look for spells. They rely on their powers so completely, that magic becomes a crutch. Which proves two things: The first is that magic is as powerful as it is addictive, and Elders and Maji are the worst addicts of all. The second is that I, Samuel J. Snyvvle, am smarter than the lot of them.

I quickly stepped inside and pushed the door shut behind me. There wasn't a stitch of light in the basement, so I lit up my finger and made my way to the stairs. Once there, I doused the flame and stealthed quietly up to the door. Very slowly, very quietly, I turned the brass knob and cracked it open. My nightvision had kicked in, and the light from the coffee machine and microwave oven flooded the apartment with light. It came streaming out around me as I poked my nose inside.

All was quiet. The place seemed empty. To be sure, I tiptoed through the entire apartment, checking each room. Still not satisfied, I checked the closets and under all the furniture. Only then could I be sure that nothing had been disturbed. Which, in itself, was disturbing. Why would someone break into my apartment and touch nothing?

The answer was obvious. Whatever they were there for, it was in the office. That meant they couldn't have been looking for the ledger. If they had been, they would have torn the place apart. I could only conclude that the intruder or intruders had broken in looking for something else; probably looking for me specifically, maybe to kill me. That would have been in keeping with everything I knew about Pretty Boy's gang. He's put more than one person on the bottom of the lake with a pair of concrete shoes. I've heard he's got other ways of getting rid of people, too. Rumor has it he even performed an *extraction* once, the worst possible thing you can do to a fae creature. It essentially turns us into ghosts, forever and ever.

There was only one way to find out. I cautiously stepped out into the hall and climbed the stairs. At the landing, I paused to examine the door to my office. I bent down, studying the bronze lock under the multi-faceted crystal knob, and saw the telltale scratches of an amateur lock-picker. They were faint. I could tell from his handiwork that the intruder knew what he was doing. He had probably had that lock open in less than thirty seconds. Then again, it's an old lock, and a true pro wouldn't have left so much as a scratch. That was a tip off. Whoever it was, he was a criminal, but not a mastermind by any stretch.

A FOOL THERE WAS

Prepared for the worst, I pulled out my taser and then gripped the door handle with my left hand. I twisted the knob. It was unlocked. A smile came to my lips. That confirmed my suspicions about the intruder's intelligence. Whenever you break into someone's office, you *lock the door* again on your way out. Otherwise, they'll know you've been there.

I gently pushed the door open, and found the office dark and empty. By all appearances, it was just as I'd left it. The hairs rose on the back of my neck. I turned slowly, scanning every inch of the room. I reached out with my senses, noting the glare of the streetlights on the furniture, the sound of the wind brushing up against the windows. I smelled cigar smoke and the faint odor of alcohol, and the smell of dust and mildew muddled in with it. And something else. Something *plasticky*.

Very slowly and carefully, I began to walk around the room. I paid close attention to the rug in the middle of the hardwood floor. I stepped off to the side and flipped it over, checking for an explosive device or a spell. Nothing.

I searched the pullout sofa, the curtains, and the desk... and that was where I hit pay dirt. Someone had wired a bomb to the bottom of my desk.

Chapter 7

The bomb was mounted high in the back, up in the narrow space behind the center desk drawer. I traced the wires up along the inside corner, behind the drawers and down to the phone cord. The wannabe killer had spliced the wires together and linked them into the triggering device on the bomb. All I had to do was pick up the phone and dial, and that'd be the end of me.

I started by unplugging the phone from the jack, just to be sure. I didn't want somebody ringing in and accidentally setting the thing off in my face. I rolled onto my back and spent the next ten minutes very carefully extracting the device. Once it was all disconnected, I found a screwdriver and released the clamp that held the bomb under my desk. At last, I placed the device on my desk for closer inspection.

I know a thing or two about bombs. Blowing things up is second nature to a goblin. When you think about it, it only makes sense. If you want to take out an enemy, and you want to do it with a minimum risk to yourself (of course), you have two choices: get someone else to do the dirty work for you, or blow the person up safely, from miles away. It's the perfect fit for an upwardly mobile goblin, or anyone else with the ruthless ambition to blow someone to smithereens. The bomb has an additional benefit: you blow up all the evidence, so no one can ever prove who did it. Not that I'm confessing anything. I'm just saying, it can be a good thing to know...

I went over the bomb and what I found didn't impress me. It was a very simplistic device. No timer or secondary trigger. Nothing at all elaborate. Just a blasting cap and a small metal ammo box full of high explosive. Simple, but effective. Any minor electrical charge -like an incoming call on the landline- would have been enough to detonate the device.

Heck, the static discharge of walking on carpet could have done the job. Whoever had placed that device in my office was lucky he hadn't blown himself up in the process. It didn't strike me as the work of a true professional. That only left about thirty thousand possible suspects in the undercity. In my head, I had a picture of Moose and his forty-five wielding goblin buddy from the parking garage. It seemed like their kind of handiwork; equal parts dangerous and dangerously incompetent.

I removed the blasting cap, rendering the device relatively harmless. With that handled, I had to face the fact that I needed to lay low for a few days. It wasn't safe to stay in my apartment until the whole thing blew over. I may have outsmarted Pretty Boy's gang once or twice, but eventually they'd catch up to me. Or worse yet, Pretty boy's brother Skully.

I only knew Skully Marcozi by reputation, but that was enough to send a chill crawling down my spine. Skully's violent exploits were the stuff of legends. They made Pretty Boy's work look like child's play. I started packing.

I packed a few clean shirts, a box of cigars, and a fifth of Scotch. I don't mind laying low, but there's no reason to rough it. I loaded the luggage into the car and tossed the bomb in

A FOOL THERE WAS

the back seat, right next to Moose's tommy gun and the two pistols. I glanced at the clock on the dash. It was just after six a.m. Too late for a goblin my age to still be awake. I needed some sleep. I needed some time to sort things out. There were far too many questions rattling around in my brain to give any one the attention it deserved.

I took an old forgotten backroad through the Canal District, heading north under the Golden Gate. The Canals are a tough place, the kind of place even the cops won't go. The district is full of bloodthirsty cutthroats and vicious gangs. Real scumbags. Fortunately, everybody knows me and I have a certain reputation among the real lowlifes of Baliztra. I've earned enough respect in the Canals that they always let me pass. Plus, they recognize my car, so they know not to mess with me.

I also had a machine gun and a bomb in the backseat, not that I would need it; I'm just trying to explain that a goblin has to be willing to do that sort of thing if he wants to be taken seriously. I am always willing: willing to face the fight, willing to take it to the next level at any time, willing to end it by any means necessary. That, boys and girls, is survival. That is why the gangs in the canals *don't mess with me.*

My cabin is up in the redwoods north of San Francisco. It's in the Muir Woods vicinity, high on a hill with a view of the ocean. The kind of place humans would kill for, but it's off limits to them. Unless they're hiking of course, but most mortals wouldn't have the wherewithal to hike all the way up that mountain, much less find my cabin. Of course, it helps that the place is hidden from humans by a powerful obfuscation spell. They could be standing right next to my house and not have the slightest clue it's there, or that I'm within spitting distance, sitting naked in my hot tub with a cigar and a jigger of booze.

Not that I *always* keep myself hidden. Sometimes, when the mood strikes me, I go running naked through the woods, freaking out the tourists and pinching the coeds who are out for a hike. A goblin's gotta have *some* fun. Usually, they run off in a fright. Sometimes, they follow me home. That's when the real fun begins.

I know what you're thinking: So *this* is the origin of all those horrible stories about people who go missing in the woods and are never seen again? Well, you're right, but you're also wrong. See, I don't kill those poor people. That's not the point. I just let them sort of see *too much*. I invite them into my house, maybe do some partying. They just don't know that once a human has seen too much, she can't be allowed back into the mundane world. She can never go back to being human. Fae magic has a way of *converting* people. A few weeks around us, and a human technically isn't human anymore.

The truth is, they usually don't want to go back anyways. Once you have a goblin, you never go back. Only kidding. I mean, it's true, but there's more to it than that. See, humans who have the ability to see, to follow me and to find my house... they're *looking* for something. They see through our spells because something inside is calling them forward. They long for something more. They *want* me to be there. They want a world full of goblins and elves and trolls and things they didn't learn in college.

So I invite them in, and after spending a few days around the fae, they're changed. It's not something I do to them, it's

A FOOL THERE WAS

just one of the effects of fairy magic. Once you've been around it, you're never the same. So these people, they become kindred. They get a little bit of the magic in their blood, and before you know it, they're one of us. I suppose after all that they *could* go back to the life of a human, always worrying about money and responsibilities, being pressured by people who only want to use them... but let's be honest: who would want to go back to that? Human life sucks, and my conscience is clear.

After climbing out of the bay, the old canal road winds back and forth to the top of a mountain and then branches out in several different directions. I'm not the only one with a house up there. There's a whole community of us. We're the fae who have enough money to own a second home, but not enough money to own that home up on Snob Hill, or -heaven forbid- among the humans. Most of us prefer the solitude of the woods and the ocean anyway.

I followed the narrow winding road up through the redwoods, the sound of my V8 engine rumbling through the canyons until at last I pulled into the driveway. I stepped out of the car and looked up at my cabin appreciatively.

My getaway is a two-story Tudor with cedar shingles and a redwood deck looking out over the ocean. I suppose it's not entirely *honest* of me to call it a cabin, but I don't like to make a big deal out of it. I don't want any "friends" inviting themselves up, if you catch my meaning. My cabin is *my place*. It's a place I go for solitude and introspection, maybe a little rabble-rousing, on my own terms. I don't have any spells protecting the place. I don't even bother to lock it. The community is so private that no one knows who lives up here, and unless they were really looking for it, most of the fae wouldn't ever even find it.

I dumped my luggage on the sofa and then hurried back to the deck to make sure the hot tub was running. I pulled the cover off and a beautiful cloud of steam gushed up around me. I smiled. Heaven.

The sun was rising, and the sky to the east had lightened a bit, but it barely managed to illuminate the dense fog along the Pacific. I stripped down in a hurry and settled into the churning waters. I poured a scotch, lit a cigar, and leaned back in the tub, letting my mind wander. A warm tingling feeling washed over me, and I had the sudden urge to fall asleep.

"I thought I'd find you here."

My heart damn near froze in my chest as I heard that low rumbling voice behind me. I stood up and turned around so fast I knocked my glass of whisky into the tub. For the second time in less than a day, I found myself face to face with Hank Mossberg. He was sitting back in the shadowy corner behind the barbecue. I should have seen him there, if I'd been paying more attention. I didn't know what Mossberg wanted, but if he'd gone to the trouble to follow me all the way up there, it wasn't good.

"I didn't expect company," I grumbled, trying to sound more confident than I felt. The truth was, at that moment I was more angry than afraid. *Nobody* invades my special place in the mountains. Or so I thought.

"I'm sure you weren't."

"Have a cigar," I said, a weak attempt to soothe the savage beast.

A FOOL THERE WAS

"I'm not here for small talk, *Snyvvle*." He snarled as he said my name. "I want the diamond."

"What diamond?"

"Don't play clever with me. I know you killed Pretty Boy Marcozi, and I know you took that diamond. His partner told me all about it."

"You're way off," I snapped. "Marcozi was a boss. He didn't even have a partner."

Mossberg smiled, an off-putting grimace that gave me the unsettling feeling he knew something I didn't. "I'll give you one more chance," he said. "Where's the diamond?"

"And I already told you: I DON'T HAVE IT!"

Hank leapt out of the chair and pounced on me. I saw him coming, but never expected he could move that fast. I leapt back, waves crashing up around me as I scrambled for the opposite end of the tub. My hand slapped down on the hardwood deck just as Mossberg's grip closed on the back of my neck.

I flailed wildly, splashing water high in the air for about three seconds before the world went dark. I felt the distant, surreal sensation of floating, and of the steamy heat closing in around me. I lost consciousness.

<hr />

I woke lying on my back, the hard edges of the redwood deck biting into the naked flesh of my backside. I felt fuzzy, like wandering out of a dentist's office still under the effects of anesthesia. I couldn't think clearly, and it took a few minutes for the world to come into focus. During that time, I was vaguely aware of Mossberg moving around the deck, but I couldn't tell what he was doing. I saw him lift something up close to his face, and I thought I heard him whisper the word, *"heavy."* Then he dropped the object on the deck next to me, something that looked and sounded like a rock as it settled heavily to the floor.

I blinked and took a deep breath. A red-tailed hawk flitted across the gray sky, and a breeze shook the branches high in the tops of the redwoods. The mist swirled around us...

"What happened?" I said at last.

"I got tired of your smart mouth," Mossberg grunted.

I tried to sit up, but something held me back. I glanced down and realized he had laid a towel across my naked body. I moved again, but the towel held me firmly down, like it was made out of lead six inches thick. I craned my neck far enough to see a rock sitting on the towel next to my right leg. I immediately realized that there were more of them.

I reached out with my senses, trying to identify the spell that held them in place, only to realize that there was none. They were simply rocks, nothing more. Rocks that were too stupid to realize they couldn't possibly get heavier just because an ogre told them to.

"Shit," I snarled. I twisted, struggling against the weight, groaning as the towel held me fast. Hank pulled up a chair and sat there, grinning down at me.

"I have all day," he said with a smirk as he poured himself a scotch and lit one of my cigars. He took a puff, and blew a large smoke ring that went floating up into the branches. He looked at the cigar appreciatively, and then held up the box. "In fact, I may have a lot more time than that," he said. He began counting the cigars. I took a deep breath.

A FOOL THERE WAS

"I already told you, I don't know where that diamond is. I don't even know what happened to Pretty Boy. By the time I got there, he was dead and the safe had already been cracked."

Hank grinned. "Now we're getting somewhere."

"So let me go. That's all I know."

"Not just yet." He leaned closer, gazing down into my face. "I still don't know why you were there in the first place." I twisted. I was starting to feel a bit claustrophobic.

"I was on a job," I said defensively.

"What job?"

"That's privileged information. I don't have to tell you that."

"I don't think so. You gave up any right to privilege when you fled the scene of a murder. I've got half a mind to haul you back to the tree and file charges against you."

"But you know I didn't do it," I groaned. He chuckled.

"Maybe. But I also know better than to trust anything that comes out of a goblin's mouth. Especially a two-bit hood like you."

"You're one to talk. Running around like a bigshot, playing Steward when nobody even believes in Stewards anymore. Look at you, Mossberg. You're not even *green*. You're a *zebra!*"

That got him. I saw the faintest glimmer of pain in his eyes, and a smirk came to my lips. Then I saw his fist close, and my eyes widened. I struggled wildly as he leaned in to take a swing at me.

"Sure, go ahead!" I shouted. "All you cops are the same. Beating up poor helpless victims. What're they gonna say when they find out? What'll they say when they see what you did to me, and they all know I wasn't even a suspect? I'll sue! I'll ruin you, Mossberg!"

He hesitated, considering my words. I took a deep relieved breath; sure that I'd just saved my own life. He shook his head.

"No," he said flatly. "Nobody can know. Not if I kill you." He raised his fist in the air and roared like a lion. I squeezed my eyes shut and squealed like a little girl. I felt a warm trickle of pee on my inner thigh.

It took a few seconds to realize Hank hadn't hit me. I quit screaming and very cautiously opened one eye. Hank was staring down at me, grinning. He threw his head back and roared with laughter. My gaze flitted to the trees, to the towel, and back to Hank.

"Not funny," I said breathlessly.

"You should be where I'm standing," he bellowed.

Hank tossed the cigar into the hot tub and swallowed the last gulp of my whisky. Then he tossed the glass in the hot tub, too. "I'm watching you, Snyvvle," he warned. "You'd better not be keeping something from me, or I'll found out. When I do, I'll come for you, and next time... it won't be so *pleasant.*"

He turned away and headed for the stairs down the side of the house, leading back to the driveway. I sighed with relief, but then realized I still couldn't move.

"Wait!" I shouted. "What about the rocks?"

He glanced over his shoulder at me. "You're a clever goblin. You'll figure a way out."

He was wrong. I never did figure a way out from underneath that towel. The closest I came was the idea of setting the thing

A FOOL THERE WAS

on fire. That was to be a last resort, of course since I'd probably burn myself alive.

Eventually, the rocks simply returned to their normal weight. It took about an hour. In Hank Mossberg's absence, they must have forgotten to be "heavy." Of course, by then I was having panic attacks, and had completely forgotten my anger. Until I looked in the hot tub and saw the swollen chunk of cigar floating in there like a big turd. Then I remembered why I hated him.

After cleaning out the tub, I put on a bathrobe and went inside to warm up by the fire. I had a lot to think about. Thanks to Mossberg, I had another clue. Despite his incredible stupidity, the Steward had actually come through for me in that regard. Now I knew that Pretty Boy had had a silent partner, someone almost no one else knew about. I knew for a fact that the partner wasn't common knowledge because I'm well enough connected that I would have known about him. That left the question of who this secret partner was, and how I could find him.

Unfortunately, the law had connected me with Pretty Boy's murder. That meant I couldn't just go around asking people questions about him. Any friend of Pretty Boy's would either call the cops, or try to kill me the moment I showed up. I might as well have had both hands tied behind my back. There was no one I could go to for information. Unless...

I snapped my fingers. I didn't need to find one of Pretty Boy's friends. What I needed was an *enemy*. I needed someone special, someone who would have wanted him dead, but couldn't have done it themselves. But who? A grin came to my face as I realized that I already knew the answer. I settled back onto the sofa, staring into the fireplace as I formulated my plan.

"Soon," I whispered under my breath. "Very soon..."

I would have all the answers.

Chapter 8

Her name was Sheba. Sheba Barsto-Marcozi. Of Pretty Boy's three wives, she had been the second. Their splashy, well-publicized divorce had redefined the term "nasty." Sheba had taken half of everything, and probably more. She took everything she could get her hands on. Pretty Boy lost millions of dollars, real estate, even businesses.

There were rumors that Sheba had hired a hitman to kill Pretty Boy. The plot had failed when Pretty Boy doubled the hitman's price and gave him a job dealing cards in one of his many casinos. At least that was the cover story. He probably had the goon doing the same thing he had been doing all along: burying secrets, along with the bodies of those that held them.

After that, things got even worse when Pretty Boy turned around and married Sheba's sister Nyva, his current wife. If anyone knew the ins and outs of Pretty Boy's relationships, it was Sheba. And if anyone wanted him dead, but couldn't do it herself, that was also Sheba. She'd have the information I needed.

Not today, though. It was time for sleep. I finished off my drink and headed for bed, somewhat lightheaded from the morning's experiences, but feeling good about myself nonetheless. I pulled the shades, slid between the silk sheets, and went out like a light.

My eyes snapped open at four p.m. It was early, still bright outside. That was good. It meant my internal clock was still working just fine. I never use an alarm clock. Alarms are for weak-willed creatures like humans and centaurs. And ogres. Any creature that sleeps so soundly it needs an alarm to wake is just asking for something bad to happen. Maybe it's a result of the way goblins are raised (or *not raised,* to be more accurate), or perhaps because of the dog-eat-dog childhoods we share. We're all light sleepers, and most of us are highly self-disciplined. That's one good reason that goblins run the world, economically speaking. Our culture requires us to be motivated self-starters. Those who aren't end up dead.

I fixed myself an omelet for breakfast. After stealing from -and working in- restaurants for all those years, I have a highly developed appreciation for quality food. Most goblins *like* good food, but they'll eat just about anything. Mostly, they just like to spend a lot of money on expensive restaurants so they can impress beautiful women or business partners. With goblins, it's all about appearances. That's where I differ from most of my kind. I'm a goblin of substance.

When I'm in the undercity, I'm usually too busy to eat right or to take the time to cook, so I spoil myself when I'm out of town. I can't just let a big kitchen and a fridge full of perfectly -magically- preserved food go to waste. I diced up some onion, tomato, orange bell and mushrooms. I spread them lightly over the center of my omelet and then spiced it up with a sprinkling of feta cheese, salt, and pepper.

I closed it up, flipped it once, and enjoyed it with a glass of sparkling white wine and a sprig of parsley. It was a breakfast

A FOOL THERE WAS

that most restaurants would have charged an arm and a leg for. That's how every meal should be.

After breakfast, I headed for the shower. I kept the bedroom curtains open so I could admire the view of the sunset. It was turning out to be a beautiful evening. The fog had pulled back from the coast, but it was looming like a ribbon of darkness in the distance. In an hour, San Francisco would be awash in fog so dense a person couldn't see five feet. It would have been a perfect night to go prowling, if I didn't have work to do. Sometimes I wish I wasn't so disciplined. After getting dressed, I lit a stogie, climbed into my car, and headed back to the real world. You know, the one with all the gnomes, goblins, and unicorns.

Half an hour later, I was back in the undercity. It was a beautiful evening. A few rays of red-hued sunlight came beaming down through holes in the ceiling of the cavern, splashing across the rooftops and illuminating the mist with an unearthly glow. To the south, across the lake, I could see tendrils of fog leaking down from above like long white fingers reaching down into the cavern, stretching towards the city. Just like topside, it was going to be a foggy night in Baliztra.

I didn't need to look up Sheba's address because it had been all over the papers a few years earlier. She lived in *The Wall*. It's a tall cliff north of the Downtown district. It's covered by homes built right into the stone. Balconies thrust outward, hanging over the precipice, offering their owners the best views money can buy.

The lights are always on up there: balcony lights, warm yellow light that cascades out of living rooms and bedroom windows, strands of colored lights strung along the balconies and facades of billionaire's homes. It's like a combination of the Mesa Verde cliff dwellings, a Manhattan skyscraper, and the French Quarter.

That's The Wall. That's where Sheba had moved after the divorce, and not just in a condo, either. She owned an entire level. She had tastes at least as expensive as her deceased ex-husband. I had to wonder if she had been spending all that money so carelessly for her own benefit, or just to piss him off. It wouldn't be the first time I'd seen a woman do that. *Hell hath no fury?* That's an understatement. At any rate, that was where Sheba had gone to spend Pretty Boy's money, and that was where I was going to find her.

I parked in the garage across the street and took the catwalk over to *The Wall*. From that vantage, I could see up and down Wyvern Street and across most of downtown. Traffic was heavy. Thousands of cars lined up, bumper-to-bumper, lights flashing, horns honking... small cars, not the kind most humans drive. My Ford isn't big at all by modern standards, but it's huge compared to most of the vehicles in the undercity. The streets of the undercity are narrow by comparison. Most of the fae drive Coopers, VWs, and those tiny little cars you see in foreign films. That is, if they drive at all. Pixies and fairies can fly. Some use gyrocopters and ultralights to get around.

As I crossed the catwalk, the glass doors magically parted ahead of me and soft classical music began to drift up from the floor. The scent of flowers washed over me. I stepped through the doors and into a tropical paradise. I was standing on the second level, facing a waterfall that cascaded down into a jungle rainforest. The water splashed into a large pool shaped like a diamond at the bottom. I looked up and saw a dozen more

A FOOL THERE WAS

levels, each one closing in above the other, until at last there was just a glass hole in the ceiling with a view straight up to the stars. Or, in tonight's case, the fog.

I've always wondered about that. The engineers must have built a building or some sort of tower topside, so that humans wouldn't suspect what was there. The fae are quite clever when it comes to that sort of thing. It helps that we've got lots of relatives who live or work topside. It also helps that we have powerful mages who can easily brainwash humans, or even erase their memory entirely.

I circled the atrium, passing through crowds of shoppers and tourists, making my way to the elevators against the inside wall. The attendant, a goblin in a dark green bellhop uniform with gold tassels, gave me a mischievous smile. It was a bit unnerving. Almost like he knew who I was. I glanced at his nametag. It said "Wyllem Azhra – Attendant."

"Evening sir," he said. "Are you here for the wake?"

"Wake?"

"The party, sir. Ms. Marcozi's sendoff for her ex-husband."

Ouch. "Yeah, yeah," I said. "The wake. What floor?"

"Step inside please." I did, and he reached around to tap the button for the top floor. I should've known. Sheba would only buy the best with Pretty Boy's money.

"Have a nice day," he said with a wicked grin. I grinned right back. I had no idea it would be so easy getting into that place. The elevator doors slid shut and I found myself pleasantly alone. The music continued to drift out of the walls, along with the sound of falling water, rustling branches, and distant thunder. That was when it dawned on me why the goblin attendant had seemed to recognize me. It was because he did.

An entire day had passed since Pretty Boy's death. That was plenty of time for the coppers to post my face all over the news, labeling me either as a killer or a person of interest. I smacked my fist against the wall. I should've known... I should have realized just how fast it would happen. That's the downside of being nocturnal. I *need* to sleep during the day, but just because I'm down and out doesn't mean the world stops turning. The cops are a twenty-four hour supermarket. They keep going and going, round the clock, like an army of robots. Thankfully, they're just about as smart as an army of robots, too.

I left the puzzling for later as the elevator chimed and the doors opened into Sheba's living room. The place was thick with partying fae creatures. A group of attractive young females elves and dryads hovered around Dirk Stone, the famous movie star hobgoblin. He was flexing his muscles, and they were fawning over him like groupies, practically drooling on each other.

Another, larger group had gathered around the bar. They were taking turns doing jelly shots out of the navels of Kiley and Karey Marckson, the famous twin pop singers. The half-elven girls were dressed in low cut jeans and halter-tops, lying on their backs on the bar. A satyr picked up one of the shot glasses in his teeth and threw his head back, downing the sweetened shot of booze in one gulp. The crowd cheered.

I stepped around Dirk and his crowd of admirers and found myself looking down at a gnome on the edge of the sofa. He was sniffing pixie dust off the glass tabletop. He snorted it

A FOOL THERE WAS

up, shivered, and then shot me a glazed look with pupils the size of Frisbees.

"Want some?" he said with a grin.

"Maybe later," I said. "Have you seen Sheba?"

He nodded towards the hall. "She's having a private party back there."

"Thanks," I said.

That's the thing about pixie dust. It's an equal opportunity drug. It can be shot, smoked, snorted, even eaten. And it has a different effect on everybody. Gnomes get a rush like humans do from cocaine, but delvers and dwarves hallucinate. Goblins just get mean. Meaner, I should say. Problem is, the stuff is highly addictive and fairly toxic. Addicts usually end up dead within a year or two. Humans who try pixie dust are usually dead within forty-eight hours. It's nasty stuff.

The door at the end of the hall was slightly ajar, and I heard raised voices inside.

"I don't care about that!" a woman said loudly. "I just want my money! No, that's not all. Think about the taxes! What about insurance? I want everything. Everything."

I'd heard enough. I pushed the door open and stepped inside. Sheba hardly glanced at me as I appeared in her bedroom. She was pacing back and forth, clutching a cell phone to her ear, screaming at someone I could only assume was an incompetent employee. I had a good chance to look her up and down while I was waiting.

Sheba had long auburn locks with loose curls at the ends and big violet eyes. She must have been half dryad and half wood-elf, or something similar. She was thin, just a few inches taller than me, and wore a light purple evening gown that showed everything she wanted it to, which was almost everything. She was a looker with a body worth writing home about, but I was tired and didn't know how to type.

She strode back and forth across the room, yammering into the phone, oblivious to everything else. She ignored the furniture, the massive poster bed, the hot tub steaming out on the patio, and me. She especially ignored me. I let her go on for another minute before I lost patience. Then I walked up to her while she had her back turned, ripped the phone out of her hand, and said into it:

"Sheba's gotta go. She'll call you back."

I ended the call and handed her the phone. She stared at me, her face a wild mix of emotions. Horror, rage, confusion. She was flustered, and I thought I'd finally managed to render her silent. I was wrong.

"Who do you think you are, hanging up on my mother like that?" she demanded. My eyebrows shot up.

"That was your mother?"

"Of course! Who else would I look to for consolation at a time like this?"

"I don't know. Your stock broker?"

"I already called him. What exactly do you want, Mister..." It was then that she took a good look at me for the first time and, to my surprise, she recognized me. "Sam! Sam Snyvvle!"

"That's my name, sweetness. Don't wear it out."

Her face lit up and she threw her arms around me. "I don't know what to say! I can't thank you enough. What do you want? Tell me, anything."

It wasn't hard to read her thoughts. She'd seen the news reports. She thought I'd killed Pretty Boy, and she was grateful

A FOOL THERE WAS

for it. She was a looker, and as I stared up into her eyes, I found the old goblin sex drive wiping my mind like a ten-year-old computer hard drive. I had to say something quick before I started to babble.

"We've got time for all that later," I said, glancing at her hot tub on the balcony. "For now, I have a few questions."

"Of course! What do you want to know?"

"Who was Pretty Boy's partner?"

"Gordy Pishard."

"Who?"

She walked over to the bar and set out two tumblers. "What do you like?"

"I'll show you sometime. For now, I'll take a scotch. About this Gordy character?"

"He's a trollog," she said, filling the tumblers with ice. "You know, the thin pale guys that look like zombies. White hair, black eyes..."

I nodded, and glanced at the tumblers. "Hold the ice," I said. "Save it for the soda pop."

She arched an eyebrow. "Tough guy, eh?"

"Maybe. What's he do?"

"Gordy? He's an inventor. According to my sources, he and Pretty Boy have been working on a special project."

"What kind of project?"

"How should I know? I may have spies, but I'm not the N.S.A."

"Touché. Do you think he might have wanted Pretty Boy dead?"

She frowned. "Why would you ask that? You *are* the one who killed him, aren't you?"

"I'm askin' the questions," I snapped. She handed me my glass and I took a swig. It was good. I made a mental note to find out what label it was so I could get my hands on some later. She had plenty I wanted to get my hands on.

"I do know that Pretty Boy provided all of Gordy's funding. I can't see how he would have benefitted by losing that. What exactly is it you're looking for?"

"Somebody wanted Pretty Boy dead," I said. I quickly added, "Somebody besides me. I want to know why. I want to know what they were after."

"I wish I could help you Sam, but all I can say is that *most* of the people I know wanted to kill him. Pretty Boy had lots of enemies, and I went out of my way to make friends with all of them. And believe me, I have plenty of friends. But as far as I know, his death shocked everyone just as much as me. You know what that means, don't you?"

"What?"

"Out of all those friends, you just made it to the top of the list."

"Lucky me."

"Yes," she said, leaning in to kiss me on the nose. "Very lucky."

I pushed her away. I had to get out of there. If I didn't do it now, I might never get out.

"Am I too much woman for you?" she taunted.

"It's just business, that's all. Where can I find this Gordy character?"

"He works in a lab, down by the docks. Mystic Synergetics."

"Thanks, dollface." I turned to leave, but she caught me by the arm.

A FOOL THERE WAS

"That's it?" she said. "I offered you anything you want, and you're just going to walk out of here?"

"I might be back," I said.

"I might not be here."

I smiled and pulled down the brim of my hat. "Sure ya will, dollface. You'll be here."

She grinned and took a sip of her drink. "I'll keep the hot tub warm."

The door opened behind us, and I turned to see a lovely violet-haired creature who almost could've been Sheba's twin except Sheba was shorter and had auburn hair and rounder curves. The woman looked familiar, but it took a second to place her. I'd seen her before. I'd seen her in the pictures in Pretty Boy's flat. She was his wife. The new one, Nyva Barsto Marcozi.

Nyva looked me up and down, and rushed into her sister's arms. I had the bizarre realization that I might be looking at the only two women in the whole undercity who shared the same married name *and* the same maiden name.

"Sam, this is my sister Nyva," Sheba said. "She's been out of town, vacationing in the Alps."

I shook her hand. "I'm sorry about your loss, Miss Marcozi."

"Thank you. I came back as soon as I heard. This is all just such a shock…" She trailed off as she stared into my face, and I could see her putting two and two together. If I gave her another minute, she'd figure out I was the guy being blamed for her husband's death. She frowned. "What did you say your name was?"

"Tardy," I quipped. "I've got business to attend to. Pleased to make your acquaintance." I headed for the door and heard Sheba call out behind me:

"Keep in touch, Sam."

I hurried out of there before things got any more complicated. I ignored the partygoers on the way out. I took the elevator back to the second floor. When I stepped out, I found the goblin attendant Wyllem still there. Once again, he was grinning at me like the cat that ate the canary. I looked him up and down.

"How was the party?" he said.

"Friendly. Is this elevator the only way in or out of this place?"

"There's a service elevator in the back, but the celebs don't use it. They *like* to be seen going in and out of here, if you know what I mean."

I reached into my pocket and produced a fifty. "Do me a favor, Wyllem," I said, handing it to him. "Let me know if Sheba Barsto goes anywhere. Here's my card. My cell number's on the bottom."

"Sure thing."

"Thanks. If you do good, there plenty more where that came from."

"Yes, sir. Is there anything else I can do for you?"

"I'll let you know."

It was easy pushing his buttons, because I'd been there before. You can always tell a goblin on his way up. They're hungry. They're *starved*. They'll take any job; do anything for a buck. Throwing him a fifty so casually like that let Wyllem know I was important, and that I could be a stepping stone

A FOOL THERE WAS

to the place he wanted to be, if he played his cards right. I expected him to do just that. I could tell he was smart. I wouldn't have been surprised if he ended up in charge of *The Wall* in a few years. In the meanwhile, he'd do anything to put another dollar in his pocket, and I was happy to help. Goblins understand the mutual benefit of certain business propositions.

It should've taken twenty minutes to get down to the docks, but it took two and a half hours. Somebody somewhere had an accident. I have no idea who or how. By the time I got there, all that was left was a plastic fender and some broken glass on the side of the road, and a few glistening specks of gold powder that the cleanup crew had missed. That was a sobering revelation. Somebody had died, right there in the middle of that road, probably with people watching. Somebody had died while I was waiting for traffic to clear so I could get back to work. I wondered how many other people had been in a hurry to get back to work, or school, or some other important thing that ultimately wouldn't mean much at all if they happened to be the poor guy lying in the middle of the road.

On the other hand, nobody in this city is innocent. For all I knew, the poor bastard deserved just what he got. There wasn't any use worrying my conscience over it. I finally got to the docks around nine p.m. I drove up and down Lakeside Road until I found the place Sheba had been talking about. Mystic Synergetics was a two-story concrete building with a sign on the wall that read "MysticS," with a yin-yang logo in purple and yellow. The building's designer had tried to dress it up with a lot of glass and some fancy planters out front, but it still just looked like a concrete box.

More and more, I see that sort of thing in the undercity. It's the influence of the humans. They don't have any discrimination. Architecture isn't important to humans anymore. Men could be building castles and cathedrals like they once did, but instead they choose to make concrete blocks and call them works of art. It's sad, really. As an appreciator of great and valuable art, it worries me that in a few more centuries, things like art and architecture won't exist anymore. Not even in the undercity. The world needs a renaissance more than ever, but I'm afraid that by the time it comes, there won't be anything left to save. On the bright side, I'll be dead by then.

I climbed the stairs and went inside. The receptionist at the front desk was a doe-eyed gnome girl with spiked pink hair and matching fingernails. She glanced at me over the rims of her glasses and then went back to typing. I stepped up to the counter and realized it was a bit taller than me. The gnome girl was two feet tall and she could barely reach the desktop. The counter loomed up in front of me, and the girl vanished.

"I'm looking for somebody," I said, raising my voice so she could hear it over the counter between us.

"Who said that?"

"Whaddya mean? I said it, lady. You just saw me come in."

"Oh." I heard a scuffling noise, and her face appeared over the counter. "Take a step back, sir."

I did, and found her standing on the reception desk. "I'm lookin' for Gordy Pishard," I said.

"You and everybody else."

"What's that mean?"

"Six months with no visitors and today everybody wants to talk to Gordy."

A FOOL THERE WAS

"Like who?"

She arched an eyebrow. "Who are you?"

"Sam."

"Do you have an appointment?"

"No, but I have this..." I reached into my jacket and flashed her my badge. She squinted her eyes.

"That's not real."

"The hell it's not."

"I'm going to call the cops."

I stiffened. I had to start talking faster.

"Look, I don't need an appointment. Gordy's an old friend of mine. I just did him a favor, a really big favor, kapish?"

She looked me up and down. I was gambling that she'd heard about Pretty Boy's death, and had probably seen or heard of me in connection with the murder. I had just implied that Gordy was connected with it, too. On the other hand, if she didn't know anything about it, she was still risking Gordy's wrath by turning away an old friend. My mind-trick paid off.

"Basement," she said, rolling her eyes towards the stairwell.

"Thanks."

I disappeared down the stairs, followed by the echoing sound of her hot pink nails tapping the keyboard furiously. I came to a blue steel door at the bottom of the stairs and glanced through the window. I saw rows of tables, lab equipment, dozens of computer workstations, and tall metal filing cabinets. I didn't see a single person anywhere. That was strange. I could have sworn she'd said Gordy was down there, and that he had guests with him. It occurred to me that the secretary may have sent me down there to buy time while she called the cops.

No, I told myself, that was just being paranoid. Gordy was in there somewhere. Maybe he'd stepped into the little trollog's room to drain his dilly. I pushed the door open.

"Gordy?" I called out. "You in there?"

I walked into the room and took a closer look at the equipment. I couldn't help but wonder what all that stuff was for. I hadn't had the time to look into Mystic Synergetics, but I'd never heard of the company before. Obviously, they were into some kind of tech. Judging from the equipment, it could have been anything from electronics to chemical weapons. It was like Frankenstein's lab on steroids.

I heard a noise at the back of the room and instinctively reached for my taser. I was nervous, I realized. That was all. The place was so strange and empty. It was like the set of a sci-fi movie where the hero wakes up and finds everyone else in the world has vanished. It didn't help that I was half-expecting the cops to come pounding down the stairwell at any minute. I steeled my nerves and called out to Gordy again. Again, I got no answer.

There was a massive piece of machinery at the end of the room that had been hidden by all the other equipment. It came into view as I stepped around a large hydraulic press. The thing was tall, at least eight feet, and it looked like a massive steel spider with trusses shaped like long steel legs stretching down to the floor. The center of the thing, the spider's torso, was an orb that looked like a large chrome ball with a spike attached to the bottom.

I heard a moan and drew my gaze to a dark mass in the far corner.

A FOOL THERE WAS

"Gordy?" I said. No answer. I rushed over, but as soon as I saw the pool of viscous steel-gray blood around the body, I knew I was too late. As I got closer, I could see the bruises on his face and the stab wounds on his chest. Then I noticed his fingers and felt my stomach twisting into knots. Gordy had been tortured.

I knelt down next to him, and Gordy cracked open his large black eyes.

"Ox," he croaked, or something like it. I couldn't make out the word, so I leaned in closer.

"Ox?" I repeated. "What ox? What do you mean?"

He coughed, and slimy gray blood poured over his lips. "Ox," he said, his voice just the faintest trace of a whisper. I leaned closer, my long pointed ear pressed right up to his mouth.

"Box... lock... box."

"Lockbox?" I said, pulling away. "What lockbox? Is that what you mean?"

His body gave one last shudder and went completely still.

Chapter 9

I turned away, confused, angry. I couldn't understand what would have made someone do that to him. I didn't know Gordy. For all I knew he had it coming... but no, nobody had *that* coming.

He'd been tortured. Slow, agonizing, purposeful. It's one thing to kill a person. Sometimes it's justice, sometimes revenge, other times it's just expedient. But it should always be quick. Every living creature knows you don't draw it out like that. You don't make the victim know he's gonna die no matter what, and just keep hurting him. That's wrong, even for a goblin. It made my blood boil.

I stepped away from the body and tried to take stock of the situation. Gordy had whispered the word "lockbox." Maybe that was why someone had killed him. Maybe he'd hidden something in a lockbox and refused to tell them. Maybe it was the diamond!

I turned, and immediately noted the row of lockers lined up against the inside wall. I hurried over and started checking them. I was surprised when I pulled the first handle and realized it was unlocked. I peeked inside and found it empty. I tried another, and found the same.

I forced myself to open each and every locker, even though I knew deep down that this wasn't what Gordy had meant. He wouldn't have gone to the trouble of concealing the diamond in an unlocked locker. That wouldn't make any sense. In fact, he hadn't even used the word "locker." It was "lockbox." I was sure of it.

I only had about ten lockers left to check when I heard the wail of sirens in the distance. I grimaced. *That's twice in twenty-four hours,* I thought. *Twice you've been the last person seen with a dead man...*

I rushed to check the last few lockers and came up empty. I turned to head for the staircase, but something stopped me. It was a thought in the back of my head... just a curious notion. I rushed back to Gordy's body. I knelt down next to him and saw that he was already in a state of decay. His white complexion had faded to ash gray, and I saw sparkles dancing off his skin like a wet match trying to ignite, but not quite managing it.

"Sorry about this, pal," I said. I reached into Gordy's jacket pocket. The instant I touched him, Gordy collapsed into a pile of sparkling gold dust. I suppressed my disgust and continued searching, digging through his pockets one by one. I found a wallet, a set of keys, half a turkey sub in a plastic bag... and then I found *the key.*

I knew what it was for the instant I laid eyes on it, because I had used one before. It was a storage key from the tram station downtown. There was also a second key on the ring, a smaller one made of black steel. That, I presumed, would open the lockbox.

By that time, the cops had arrived. The sirens went quiet as they pulled into the parking lot and entered the building. It was too late to get out of there without being seen. The stairwell was out of the question. I searched for alternatives.

A FOOL THERE WAS

I figured I could set a fire and hope that would distract the coppers as I made my escape. It was the same trick I'd used back at Pixieland, and it had worked pretty good then. Or, I could try climbing out one of the narrow windows along the top of the wall. Maybe both...

I noticed a fire alarm switch on the wall and realized that would be just as helpful, and less work. I smashed the glass with my elbow and yanked down the thin metal handle. The siren came to life with an ear-shattering screech.

I leapt onto one of the workstations against the outside wall and pulled myself up. I was staring into a culvert below the level of the outside lawn. All I saw was the bright reflection of flashing blue and red lights. Not having much choice in the matter, I pushed the window open and climbed through. I could just barely fit into the tiny opening, and I had to swing my legs side to side in order to squeeze through.

Behind me, I heard shouting as the cops busted into the lab. I was sure they must have seen me. I twisted in the narrow culvert and spun around to see a team of elves and hobgoblins in blue uniforms moving through the laboratory, tazers drawn, flashlights blazing. They were shouting back and forth to each other, but their gas masks muffled the sound. I couldn't make out a word.

I gently lowered the windowpane back into place. Then I turned around to risk a peek up over the edge of the culvert, across the lawn. I saw six squad cars, a van, and two ambulances. Two fire trucks were coming down the road. Either it was my imagination, or the cops had come there knowing somebody was hurt. That confirmed at least that someone had called them; someone who knew about Gordy.

I'd have given my right arm to find out who dialed that number. Maybe not my whole arm, but definitely a finger or two.

I saw figures passing back and forth across the lawn in front of the lights. Cops, medical workers, firefighters. Everybody was getting a piece of the action. I waited for an opportune moment and then jumped out of the culvert. With the practiced expertise only a goblin can boast, I melded into the shadows and tiptoed out of there without so much as drawing a glance.

I hadn't gone far when I realized I was without a vehicle. I hadn't been expecting this sort of trouble. I had parked in the laboratory parking lot, right out front. My hotrod was now blocked in by all those police vehicles and fire trucks. I could have kicked myself. Now, they'd know for sure that I had been there, and on top of it all, they would probably impound my car.

I was getting deeper into it by the minute, and I was floundering. I didn't have the slightest idea who might have killed Pretty Boy and taken that diamond. I could only guess that it was the same person who'd killed Gordy, but for reasons I couldn't yet fathom. The only clue I had in the whole world was the small iron key in my pocket, and it didn't feel like much.

I crossed the highway and started the hike back downtown. I had half a mind to use my cell phone to call a cab, but I didn't want to be seen in that neighborhood. I could always explain away the presence of my car, but a cab driver would be one more person to I.D. me at the scene. When it comes to legal matters, every piece of evidence is vital. Every piece of evidence

A FOOL THERE WAS

that the cops *don't* have, is something a good lawyer can use against them. I'd elaborate on how I know this information, but I think you can figure it out.

I found a tram station at the edge of the business district. It was a seedy little stop, full of homeless beggars and *Greenskin* gang members. I had to stare down half a dozen people before I even bought a ticket. Thankfully, I only had a few minutes to wait for the tram. Otherwise, I might have had to pick somebody out to make into an example.

That's how it works in the mean streets. Nobody seems to understand this. You can't just walk into a seedy neighborhood and expect people to leave you alone. Criminals aren't like normal people. They're like feral dogs. They're always looking for an opportunity. Sometimes they want to prove themselves. Sometimes they want to elevate their status in the pecking order, like a dog that knows it's never going to be the alpha but still doesn't want to be the runt. Sometimes, they're just looking for an easy target.

There's only one way to prevent becoming a victim to people like that, and it's by being proactive. You pick out one of them, one who looks dangerous. Not the alpha, but maybe somebody high enough in the pecking order that the others don't mess with him. Then you beat the ever-loving hell out of him.

This usually works out okay because the Alpha doesn't care much what happens to his inferiors. He knows you're not interested in taking his place in the pack, so he finds it amusing. For him, it's entertainment, like watching brownie-fights. But the others don't know what to make of it. They just saw you beat the crap out of someone they fear and respect. That means you could do it to them, too. And they lack the intelligence or organization to band together and attack you, because they look to the Alpha for that. So they leave you alone.

Thankfully, it didn't come to that. Not that I mind beating the tar out of some random scumbag just to prove a point. Truth is, a random act of violence could only have helped my reputation, not to mention my mood. But I was running out of steam. I was getting tired of looking over my shoulder, wondering when the cops or Pretty Boy's goons would catch up to me. I was tired, my head too full of facts I couldn't seem to sort out. I just wanted to get to that lockbox and find out what it was all about.

I only had to ride the tram across town, so it didn't take long. In less than twenty minutes, I was walking around the downtown depot. I've always liked that place. It smells like food and popcorn. It has an air of excitement, like a carnival. The sounds of trams coming and going, music pumping out of the cheap tinny speakers, the bustle of a thousand easy marks rushing back and forth, too distracted by their daily routines to notice the light touch of a disappearing wallet as a young goblin picks their pockets.

I spent many wonderful nights there in my youth, perfecting my survival skills. There was a time when I was the fastest pickpocket in the city, and I could do it while juggling and telling jokes, too. I was shameless, perfect. Ah, the idle pleasures of youth.

I was in a hurry, so I cut through the crowd and went straight to the lockers by the ticket station. I walked up and down the rows of tall brick-red lockers until I found the number that matched the one on the key. Before opening it,

A FOOL THERE WAS

I paused to look around. I saw four long lines of people at the ticket counter: two dwarves having a conversation, a satyr in a three-piece suit on his way to work, a troll woman with three kids in tow, each trying to scream louder than the others. And one cop. Not a real cop, a security goon. This one didn't look too bad, though. He was a goblin, and he seemed more interested in the pretty wood-nymph at the counter than anything else.

Satisfied that I was alone, I jammed the key into the locker and yanked it open. I almost sighed aloud when I saw a small red lockbox inside. This was what I had been waiting for. Inside that box was the clue that would tie it all together. I couldn't wait any longer. I pulled it out of there and jammed the key into the lock. I was so nervous that I was shaking, and I nearly bent the damn thing just trying to get it in there. Then, at last, it slid into place with a clicking noise. I half expected a ray of light to shine down from heaven.

Hurriedly, I pulled the lid open. Inside, I found a single folded piece of paper. I snatched it up and then returned the lockbox to the locker. I was just removing the key when I felt something round and hard poking into my rib cage.

"Give me that key," said a gravelly voice. I turned slowly, holding out the key in one hand. As I did, I slipped the piece of paper into my pocket. I found myself staring into the eyes of the goblin security guard. He was brandishing a stainless steel wand with a ruby tip. I glanced over his shoulder and saw three more goblins, all in business suits. One of them stood out. He was taller, with thick, moss-colored hair, wearing a very expensive wool trench coat over a custom tailored silk suit. I knew immediately who this was.

"You must be Pretty Boy's brother," I said.

The security guard snatched the key out of my hand and shoved me back up against the locker. He shoved his wand into my gut and sneered threateningly.

"Name's Skully," the mobster said with a New Jersey accent. "You the mook who killed my brother?" *Mook*. That's *sharizi* for crook, or criminal. Not a smart one, though. The kind who gets his money by knocking people over the head and stealing their wallet. It's something of an insult.

"Of course not," I said, noting the fact that I'd just been personally insulted by one of the fae's most powerful criminals. I was moving up in the world. "I didn't even know Pretty Boy until I went to his house and found him there, dead."

"That's too bad. I would have wanted to shake your hand. But seeing as you're here now, breaking into my locker, and you haven't done me any kind of favors at all, I'm gonna have to kill you."

The guard twisted his wand and it shot an electrical charge right into my gut. It was like getting punched from the inside out. It knocked the breath right out of me. I double over, gasping, and they all broke out in laughter. I glanced to the side and saw the troll woman with her kids hurrying away, trying not to look in my direction.

"Why?" I said between gasps. "Why would you want to kill your own brother?" He laughed.

"Pretty Boy was a mook, like you. I just wanted him out of the picture. Pretty Boy got too full of himself. Started thinking he was better than me; that he could do things I couldn't. That little punk thought *he could use me.*"

A FOOL THERE WAS

I straightened myself up. "Pretty Boy wasn't much like you. He didn't look like you."

"I'll take that as a compliment. We're both half-human, but he looked *all* human. He got the looks, I got the sense. Nature plays these tricks. I probably should have killed him right away, but I knew we each had something to offer. Pretty Boy could manipulate people. He could charm them with his good looks and make people believe just about anything. I had other ways, goblin ways... We worked like partners, building ourselves up from nothing. I'm sure you can appreciate that."

"Goblins don't have partners," I said.

He shrugged. "Maybe we inherited that from pop, whoever he was. It doesn't matter now. Pretty Boy got too full of himself, and look where that got him." He glanced at the others. "Come on boys, let's take him to the basement."

They caught me by the arms and started to drag me away. I tried to struggle, but they lifted my feet off the ground. About that time, somebody shouted, "FREEZE!" A horde of blue uniforms appeared all around us.

Skully and his goons didn't even have a chance to put up a fight. The cops closed in on us, knocking us to the ground, and we all went down in a dogpile. Naturally, I ended up on the bottom. Suddenly, all I could see was fists and batons. There was a lot of shouting and cursing. I heard the sounds of tasers and wands going off all around me. I decided it was time to get out of there.

As the bodies pressed down on top of me, I wiggled back and forth, looking for an opportunity to make my escape. Their weight was unbalanced, shifting constantly as the mobsters tried to escape and the cops tried to wrangle them under control. I slid left and right, all the while dragging myself forward one inch at a time. As I moved, the bodies collapsed in behind me. After a few seconds, I could see flashes of daylight between the flailing arms, legs, and nightsticks.

I finally made my escape between the legs of a massive hobgoblin who didn't even have a clue I was there. I snaked out from under him and jumped to my feet. I glanced back and saw his fists rising and falling repeatedly, hammering up and down just as fast as he could swing. I couldn't help noticing that he was doing a better job of beating on the other cops than he was of hitting the mobsters. He didn't care. He was just glad for the chance to punch someone.

I rushed to the end of the row of lockers before anyone even realized I was gone. I looked back just in time to see a wood-elf halfway down the pile glance in my direction. He locked eyes with me.

"There!" he shouted. "One of them is getting away!" I grinned and took off like a rocket. I heard shouting behind me, but the sounds quickly faded as I left the ticket area and squeezed into the busy terminal.

I purposefully moved into the crowd, selecting the larger pedestrians as cover. Dwarves, hobgoblins, and centaurs all work wonderfully when utilized in this fashion. Centaurs, however, can be temperamental, and when they get jumpy, they tend to kick out behind them without checking whether someone is actually there or not. One good kick from a centaur can split a goblin's skull wide open.

A tram pulled out of the station and a few seconds later, another pulled in. I walked up behind the conductor while he was checking a fat dwarf lady's ticket, and slipped in right

A FOOL THERE WAS

behind him. I climbed the steps onto the tram, walked casually down the aisle, and took a seat on the side opposite from the traffic. That gave me a nice vantage point to look out for the cops.

Over the next few minutes, I saw a couple of them moving back and forth through the crowd, but none made it to the tram before it pulled out of the station.

At that point, the automated system took over. I was home free. The light at the front of the tram came on, announcing that our next stop was the Artisan district, west of downtown. I settled back to enjoy the ride. I leaned my head back and closed my eyes. I was tired, and I had a lot to think about...

"Hello, Sam."

I opened my eyes and looked up into the hideous upside-down face of Hank Mossberg. He was leaning over the seat behind me. I pushed to the side, trying to weasel out from under him, but his hand shot out and closed around my face. I caught him by the wrist and tried to pull myself free, but I could already feel the energy draining out of me.

I blinked once, twice... and the world went dark.

Chapter 10

On the night I was born, I learned two important lessons that would guide me for the rest of my life: Never Trust Anyone, and equally importantly, Appreciate the Finer Things. You already know how I learned the first lesson, but I owe the second all to *Antonio's,* that miraculous little restaurant where I took shelter from the evil clutches of my murderous siblings.

While the chef chased the other goblins down the alley with his broomstick, I slipped into the kitchen and took shelter in a dark corner beneath a big copper sink. From there, I could feel the warmth of the ovens and smell the heavenly aromas of pizza, pasta, and garlic bread drifting past me, up towards the window. I was famished, but too afraid to venture out of my hiding spot and risk the same treatment my siblings had received.

It was many hours later, just before dawn, when Chef Antonio finally turned off the ovens, put out the lights, and locked the doors. By then, I was hungry enough to gnaw off my own leg. The smells of cooking had overwhelmed me all night, and considering the caloric needs of a young goblin, it was a wonder I hadn't already starved.

Then, miraculously, I had the place to myself. I admit I went a bit crazy that first night. I had seen the chef and his employees coming and going throughout the evening. I was familiar with the layout of the kitchen. The easiest target was the pantry, which was really little more than a large shelf of dry goods and a few vegetables. Naturally, I helped myself to whatever I wanted.

I sampled everything, tossing aside what I didn't like, stuffing the rest down my gullet just as fast as I could eat. I consumed an entire loaf of bread, half a platter of vegetables, and drank two bottles of wine. I discarded the leftovers and less tasty samples, leaving them scattered across the floor. I dumped the entire collection of spices onto the floor. I can't even imagine what it must have cost poor Chef Antonio to refill his large jars of oregano, basil, and paprika.

When my belly was full and I was feeling somewhat drunk and quite satisfied with myself, I leisurely explored the rest of the business, looking for more trouble to get into. I found more spices on the tables out front, and a few bottles of olive oil, which I dumped. I tore a tablecloth apart, worrying it away like a puppy with a bone, and then curled up on the shredded remains for a nap.

I slept the last few hours of the day, until I heard the chef fussing with the lock on the front door at four p.m. I snapped awake and scurried back into the kitchen, out of sight. I crawled into my hiding place in the corner under the sink, but as Chef Antonio came into the restaurant and discovered my vandalism, I realized that I had better get out of there. Unfortunately, I didn't understand how to work the door. Instead, I slipped out through the window over the sink and climbed up onto the roof.

My strength had been building up, and it was an easy climb for me. The old brick wall was covered in pipes and rain ducts,

A FOOL THERE WAS

making my ascent almost effortless. Within seconds, I was up the side and over the ledge. I ducked down in the shadows and waited. I could hear the sounds of the chef's curses drifting up through the broken window. It didn't take long for me to realize that Chef Antonio had decided the goblin whelps he'd chased off the previous night had come back for revenge. He blamed everything on my siblings, and that was fine with me.

The chef called a repairman to fix the window. A truck came to haul away the ruined food. Things quieted down after midnight. I was tired, so I found an old canvas tarp wedged into a shadowy corner by the wind, and I curled up underneath it. I burrowed down deep, where the sunlight streaming down from the holes in the roof of the cavern couldn't hurt my eyes, and I fell fast asleep.

When I woke, I was once again famished. I didn't want to ruin the good thing I had with that restaurant, and I was smart enough to realize that I needed a way back inside without breaking anything. I located another window; a narrow heat exhaust high in the wall. It was difficult to reach, both inside and out, which was why the chef had left it permanently open to vent the hot steamy air out of the kitchen. I found that by climbing down a pipe and then swinging by one hand, I could just reach the windowsill with my fingertips. That was enough to get me inside.

Once I did get in, what I found inside was devastating. Antonio had closed shop, and wouldn't be open again for a week. Of course, I couldn't read the sign to understand all that. I was a newly born goblin with only a vague idea of how to communicate, much less read the sign on the front door that explained the situation to the chef's customers. As far as I could tell, the place was empty and would stay that way forever. Worse yet, the food was gone! Because of me, Chef Antonio had emptied his food stores. I had no choice but to go searching elsewhere for my next meal.

After beginning my life with some of the tastiest food in the entire undercity, I sadly found myself reduced on the second night to digging through dumpsters and piles of rubbish in the back alleys of *The Wells*. After that, most of my meals consisted of moldy bread crusts and rotting vegetables, after which I would lie awake on the roof, gazing up at the beams of daylight streaming down from above, listening to the uneasy rumblings of my tender stomach.

Goblins can eat just about anything, but after spoiling myself on the riches of *Antonio's* kitchen, I knew better than to think that someone's discarded refuse could ever make a satisfying meal. So I dreamed about pizza, pasta, and large loaves of warm, crispy bread with butter. All the while, I was eating things that were, in my opinion, not even good enough for a gutter rat. I knew that if I ever got into another situation like the one I'd had with *Antonio's,* I'd be careful not to ruin it.

Over time, I managed to improve my own means. During my adventures in the trash heaps of the undercity, I located a good wool blanket (apparently discarded because of a stain), a lantern that was severely dented but otherwise worked perfectly fine, and several boxes of books and magazines. I began to read.

I cut my intellectual teeth on *Undercity Weekly* and *Playfae*. I learned the basics and quickly moved on to more advanced studies: *The Tales of King Arthur, The Care and Feeding of Firedrakes,* and of course, *Phantastes* by George MacDonald.

A FOOL THERE WAS

But what I found most interesting were the collections of *True Crime* and *Pulp Detective Stories*. I couldn't get enough of them. When I finished reading them all, I started over. I read them a second and third time, until the covers were torn and the pages were falling out.

I was fascinated by the brooding, solitary figure of the private detective. It didn't take long to see that most of these fictional characters were cut from the same cloth. They were tough, streetwise, and dangerous. They were cynical and sometimes judgmental, blunt but passionate. They had their own way of thinking. For the private eye, it was all about solving the case. Women fawned over these loners for the same reasons I did. They were powerful. They weren't necessarily big and strong, but they were tough, and they were nobody's fools. Somewhere in the back of my mind, those stories changed me, but it would be years before I realized just how much.

In the midst of my studies, Chef Antonio returned to work. He had secured the financing necessary to reopen his restaurant, and when he fired the ovens up, I could smell the food from blocks away. I came running. I climbed up to my makeshift lean-to on the roof and waited patiently, my stomach rumbling agonizingly as the fumes of all that wonderful food came drifting up to me. I was salivating, but I tempered my anxiousness with caution. Never again would I make the same mistake.

When it was finally safe, I snuck into *Antonio's* and helped myself to a meal. But just one small meal, a few odds and ends that I was sure he would never miss. Then I left, and didn't come back until he had closed up the next day.

You see, by way of contrasts I had developed a taste for the finer things. I appreciated wine and olive oil and pesto, not just because I had enjoyed those things in the past, but because I knew what it was like to do *without* those things.

And thanks to my reading, I had also learned that there were many other fine things in life. Not everyone lived on a rooftop, for example. Some people had mattresses and beds. They also had refrigerators full of food and luxurious cars for transportation. What they really had though, were jobs. That, I was to learn, was the difference between lifestyles. Even a lowly dishwasher or busboy with a tiny apartment and only one set of clothes might enjoy a fantastic meal every day. He might even save up enough money to buy a car or a house, in time. With hard work and self-discipline, anything might be possible...

Over the next year, I grew to maturity. It's hard for humans to comprehend this, but we aren't born helpless like they are. Goblins and most other fae creatures mature quite rapidly, much the same as a puppy or kitten. By the time I was one year old, I was the equivalent of a human teenager. And, thanks to all my reading, I was probably the most sophisticated goblin in all the undercity.

All of my books and magazines had given me a thirst for knowledge, but it was Chef Antonio who gave me a taste for the finer things. That's why I went to him for my first job as a busboy. And from that day forward, I never stole from him again.

I also never forgot about those private detectives. I saved those old magazines and pulp novels to read again and again, and I bought more of them with every paycheck. I became a fan of everything from Sherlock Holmes to Sam Spade.

A FOOL THERE WAS

Eventually, I even discovered television and characters like Jim Rockford and Richard Castle. But as much as I loved reading those stories and watching those shows, it never occurred to me that I might actually become one of them.

That is, until that one fateful day, when I met Belle the bounty hunter.

Chapter 11

I'm not sure how long I was out. I woke in Hank Mossberg's jail cell. I opened my eyes and found myself staring at a ceiling of dark marbled wood. As my eyes went in and out of focus, I thought I saw the veins in the wood pulsing, like real veins in a human body. I blinked and drew my gaze away. I didn't want to know if the effect was real or imagined.

The walls of the cell were solid, carved right out of a massive root. I reached out to feel it and found that it was smooth to the touch and at least as dense as steel. The bars at the front of the cell were made of roots and vines, probably equally strong, based on stories I'd heard. The scent of moss and earth filled the place. I felt like I had been buried alive.

Mossberg was sitting at his desk in the middle of the room, playing cards with a young, clean-shaven dwarf. I rubbed my eyes and sat up slowly. I hadn't ever seen a clean-shaven dwarf before. I thought I might be hallucinating.

I very quietly stealthed up to the cell bars and tried slipping out between them. No such luck. Not only were they as strong as steel, it almost seemed like they could sense where I wanted to go, because they drew closer as I touched them.

"Have a nice nap?" the dwarf said. I glanced at him. He was grinning like an idiot. Looked more like a pig than a dwarf.

"Hey Mossberg," I said. "Who's the kid?"

The dwarf's smile vanished. He set his cards on the table and fixed me with an icy glare.

"The name's Mickey, and you'd better watch your mouth."

"Yeah, or what?"

"Or I'm gonna come over there and shut it for you."

"Come on over then, little pig. Or I'll huff, and I'll puff!"

"THAT'S ENOUGH!" Hank shouted. I swear the floor of the cave shook under my feet. Mickey damn near dropped out of his chair and I felt my bladder go terrifyingly weak. I took a step back.

"Just foolin' around," I said meekly.

Hank stomped over to the cell and looked down at me like he might be considering me as his next meal. "I think you've done quite enough *fooling around* in the last twenty-four hours. I've just about run out of patience with you, Snyvvle. I've told you twice to stay out of this mess, but every time I turn around, there you are. What have you got to say for yourself?"

"I know what it looks like," I stammered. "I had to run, Hank. It's the only way I could prove it wasn't me."

He furrowed his brow and his eyes narrowed. "Why should I believe you?"

"Because it's the truth. That's what you're all about, isn't it? Finding out the truth? Protecting the innocent?"

"Innocent? What's that got to do with you?"

"Come on, Mossberg. You can't really think I had something to do with Pretty Boy's death. That would be crazy. I ain't got a death wish. You know me, I'm a coward. Why would I sign my own hit by killing Pretty Boy?"

"I think that's the first honest thing you've said yet," Hank snapped. He wandered back over to his desk and picked up his

A FOOL THERE WAS

cards. "All right, let's hear your story." He tossed a card on the table and motioned for Mickey to deal him another. I started talking.

I had already told Hank about being hired to find the diamond, but I went over it again. I also went over my visit with Sheba and how she'd led me to Gordy's lab. Hank had already known Pretty Boy had a partner -he was the one who clued me in on that- but he had decided that there was no connection between Gordy and Pretty Boy's murder. Of course, at that point, Gordy had still been alive.

I gave Hank enough to details to make the story true, but I left out some stuff. He didn't need to know about the goons who had attacked me, or the bomb I had sitting in the backseat of my car. Then again, he might already know about that stuff. I never could be sure with Hank.

"What about the tram station?" he asked when I'd finally finished my story. "What were you looking for there?"

"Nothing," I said quickly. "I was just there to pick up some corn dogs and cotton candy."

"Is that so?" Hank said. He glanced at Mickey, and Mickey grinned from ear to ear. My stomach twisted up in knots.

"What do you mean?" I said cautiously.

I had the sinking feeling that they knew something I didn't, like they'd just pulled the rug out from under me, or worse yet, maybe they'd let me pull it out from under myself. Mickey lifted a piece of paper from the desk -one single sheet, awkwardly creased as if it had been folded carelessly and in great haste- and deliberately began to open it, very slowly and methodically, almost as if he had rehearsed this scene a thousand times. Before he even had it open, my hand was in my pocket. Sure enough, the paper I'd found in the lockbox was *gone*. Rather, it was there, across the room in Porky's fat little fingers.

"Hank, look what I found," Mickey said in a coy voice. "Gee, it looks real important." He handed the paper to the Steward, who accepted it without a glance and then shot me a look.

"I don't suppose you know anything about this?" he said.

My gears started turning. I'd never even had the chance to look at that piece of paper. From the moment I'd pulled it out of the lockbox and shoved it into my pocket, I'd been on the run. I couldn't even guess what it might say.

But Hank knew. *Cripes*, he knew and he was using it to toy with me. He was testing me. I had to think fast, but it wasn't easy. I never would have thought Hank was smart enough to play mind games with me like that. The whole situation threw me off.

It must have been the dwarf, I decided. That stupid-looking dwarf was using Hank like a ventriloquist's puppet. But that didn't change anything. The fact was, they had *my* clue. In fact, for all I knew, they might be holding the motive right there and not even know what it was. I had to get it back.

"It's my shopping list," I said. Hank didn't think it was funny. He didn't say anything, just shook his head. I was going to have to do better that. Wisecracks weren't going to cut it.

"Why are you asking me?" I said. "You have it right there. You should have figured it out by now."

They glanced at each other over their cards, and that's when I realized I'd stumbled onto something important. They *didn't* know what was on that paper. But what could that possibly

A FOOL THERE WAS

mean? They'd had hours to look it over while I was asleep in that cell. What could be on that paper that the two of them hadn't been able to figure out in all that time?

Maybe it was written in a foreign language, or some sort of code. Yeah, that would make sense. A code that Gordy had made up to protect his information. But what kind of information would he have had that was worth his life? It had to be something that could fit on a single piece of paper... but what? Maybe it had something to do with his lab? There had to be a connection there. After all, Pretty Boy was financing the place. That in itself was still a mystery. What interest would a mobster have in a high-tech lab?

I slumped my shoulders in defeat. Hank had the upper hand, and he knew it. No amount of fast-talking was going to get me out of that cell. Whatever it was that Hank wanted from me, I didn't have it. But I didn't have to let him know that.

"Let me see it," I said.

Mickey rolled his eyes.

"I'm serious. Give it to me, and I'll show you what it means."

Mickey glanced at Hank, and Hank shrugged. He didn't care if I saw it. He knew I wasn't going anywhere. Mickey snorted his disapproval, but still followed the instructions. He brought the piece of paper over to me, and I snatched it out of his hand as soon as he was in reach. I glanced over it as I wandered to the back of the cell. I frowned. What I had wasn't a code or a foreign language at all... it was a blueprint.

"Well?" Mickey demanded.

I glanced at him and then back to the paper, wondering how much I should tell them. I considered playing dumb, but

I knew that wouldn't get me anywhere. Especially since they would both know the truth in a few hours, or a day at the most. For the moment however, it was obvious that they didn't know who had owned that lockbox. They may not have even heard about Gordy's death. That would explain why they hadn't connected him to the blueprint.

"It's a blueprint of a machine."

"Well, obviously," said Mickey. "What's the machine do?"

I handed the paper back to him. "I can't say... but I *can* show you where it is." Mickey's eyes widened, and he glanced at Hank.

The ogre rose out of his chair and stretched impressively. He raised his arms over head and his hands disappeared into the roots. His back popped with the sound of a falling tree. He took a deep breath, inflating his chest like a hot air balloon, and then let it out in a sigh. He relaxed and stood there, glaring at me.

"Where is it?"

"I'll show you."

"No, I don't think so. As soon as I let you out of there, you'll try to escape."

He had a point.

"Hardly," I lied. "I wouldn't get ten feet with the two of you watching me. Besides, I think I might know how the thing actually works. But I can't be sure unless I'm there."

"What difference does it make?" said Hank.

I could see the gears turning in that thick skull of his. He was trying to make the connection between me, that paper, and the mobsters who were trying to take it from me. From his

A FOOL THERE WAS

perspective, nothing made sense. And he didn't know the half of it. I tried to hide my smile. I still had the advantage.

"If we can figure out what it's for," I said helpfully, "that might be the evidence we need to put Skully Marcozi behind bars."

"Marcozi?" Hank said. "Pretty Boy's brother? That's who that was at the depot?"

Oops. I'd played my hand prematurely. That was okay. I still had plenty of aces up my sleeve. And jokers, too. Never discount the joker.

"In the flesh," I said. "He wanted that blueprint bad, but I beat him to it. If the coppers hadn't showed up when they did, I'd be swimming in the lake with concrete shoes right now. In fact, that blueprint might even be the reason Pretty Boy was killed..."

Hank ruminated on that. *What was this new angle*, he was wondering. Had Pretty Boy truly been murdered over that blueprint? Why was it so important? Hell, I'd have given any one of my four testicles to know the answer to that question.

Hank reached out, letting his fingertips graze the roots at the front of the cell, and they went limp. I stepped through with a big smile on my face. I had won. Hank reached into his pocket and pulled out a pair of silver cuffs, the kind that neutralize fairy magic.

"Put these on," he said.

I considered putting up a fight, but decided it wasn't worth it. All that would do was cost me time, and I didn't have much time to waste. Maybe the cops were holding Skully, but it was only a matter of time before he was back on the streets. After all, he hadn't broken any laws that I knew of. He had goons for that. As usual, the mob boss would come out smelling like a rose. And within a few hours, he'd be gunning me down in a pool of green blood. No, I definitely didn't have any time to waste. I obediently slipped on the cuffs and started for the tunnel.

"Right this way, boys," I said, and they fell in behind me.

I led Hank and his pet dwarf down the corridor to the tram depot, a quick ten minute walk. We hopped the tram and rode it up to the Lakeside stop, the same seedy place I'd been a few hours earlier. It was an uncomfortable trip. I didn't bother trying to conceal the handcuffs, and because of that, I got a lot of looks. Several people got up and moved to the end of the tram, trying to keep a safe distance from me, an obvious criminal.

Somebody was bound to recognize me and take a snapshot with his smartphone, but I wasn't worried about that. Within a few hours, word would be out that I'd been arrested by the Steward. That would lead to speculation of course, and curiosity. By the end of the day, it would be all over town: *Sam Snyvvle, P.I., arrested in connection with a murder!*

Heck, I might even get on the news. That would be fantastic. In my business, that's what they call "*word of mouth advertising.*" Even the dumbest goblin knows there's no such thing as bad publicity.

It was two a.m. when we got to the laboratory. The police had cordoned off the entire area with crime scene tape. I couldn't help noticing that my car was nowhere to be seen. Just as I'd feared, they had probably towed it. We walked up to the front doors, and I gave the handle a tug. Naturally, the doors

A FOOL THERE WAS

were locked. I looked at Hank and I could see from his frown that he wasn't sure what to do.

Obviously, there are legal issues involved with breaking into private property. Even more so, since that private property was now an official crime scene. I didn't have my lockpicks, either. Hank had confiscated those along with that blueprint. I was going to have to give him a nudge, or he'd get carried away worrying about how to handle this moral dilemma.

"It's a bust," I said. "Doors are locked. Guess we'll have to go back to the jail. Maybe next time..."

"I don't think so," Hank said. He grabbed the handle and pulled so hard that he bent both doorframes. The doors swung open, and half a dozen protection spells went off. Multicolored sparks flashed all around us like the grand finale on the Fourth of July. A thin cloud of purple smoke went drifting lazily towards the lake.

"Guess the lock was broken," Hank mumbled. He ripped the police tape and held the door open as he waved me in.

"Ladies first," Mickey said un-cleverly.

"You're one to talk. At least I can grow a beard," I snapped, stepping past him. Mickey shoved me from behind and I almost tripped. I regained my balance and shot him a glare. "Real tough guy, attacking a prisoner wearing cuffs," I said. "Smack me around a little with a billy club why don't you? Then you might even qualify to join the police force."

"Shutup," the Steward said behind us. "Get moving, both of you."

I went to the stairs and pushed the door open with my shoulder. They followed me in, and we made our way down to the basement. The place was a mess. The cops had torn the lab apart. Apparently, they had been looking for something. Maybe a clue as to why Gordy had been killed. Or maybe not. Maybe they just tore the place apart because they had an excuse. I've seen them do that sort of thing before. I led the boys to the back, and showed them the machine.

"He was telling the truth," Mickey said in awe as he held up the blueprint to compare it. "It's really real."

"Of course it is, ya mook," I said.

"And this is why Gordy was killed?" Hank said, looking the machine up and down. "How does it work?"

"Let's find out. The power switch is right there." I nodded at the big switch with the green button next to it, on the lower part of the spider's abdomen. Mickey took Hank's indifference as approval. He walked up to the switch and flipped it. There was a clicking sound followed by a low, deep hum that reverberated out of the torso. After a few seconds, the hairs on my neck stood up and I saw a tendril of lightning crawl across the shiny metal orb, down towards the spike. I took a step back.

The lightning skipped back and forth across the surface like it was skating on ice. Another bolt appeared with a loud *crack*, and they joined at the base, forming the shape of a V. I could feel the energy building in intensity, Inside the metal torso, the humming grew louder. A second later, two more tendrils appeared and joined with the others, *cracking* and arcing back and forth across the surface of the orb.

Then I noticed something: The electricity was trying to jump from the spike at the bottom of the torso, down to the floor. I followed the path to the base of the machine and saw a metal plate with a round mounting bracket about the size of a silver dollar... *or a pink diamond*.

A FOOL THERE WAS

My mind reeled as I raced for an answer to tie it all together. The obvious conclusion was that machine, whatever it was, needed that diamond to work. That was why Pretty Boy had the Scarlet Tear in the first place. And someone had killed him for it, and then they'd killed Gordy, too... or had they?

Too many things about that didn't make sense. If they'd killed Gordy looking for the diamond, why did he clue me in on the blueprints? Something about the machine itself was important. It had to be. A man doesn't use his dying breath to talk nonsense. Gordy had wanted me to find those prints. He hadn't said a word about the diamond.

Then there was Honey. How was she connected to all this, and why did she send me for that diamond? Did she know about this machine? Maybe she didn't. Maybe she really had been Pretty Boy's lover. That would explain a lot. For example, Pretty Boy may have been showing it off to her, trying to impress Honey, and then maybe she'd come up with the grand idea of stealing it. Only she couldn't do it herself, she needed a schmuck like me to do it for her.

But the murder had taken her by surprise. I'd seen her face when I told Honey that Pretty Boy was dead, and she was shocked. I believed that she was innocent, at least in that aspect. *How many people out there knew about the diamond*, I wondered. What about the machine? Gordy? He was the only third party who would have known about both. Or was he? There was Sheba... and of course, Skully Marcozi.

Skully would have had access to any information he wanted. He could have killed his brother for the diamond, and then killed Gordy for the plans to the machine. Now that almost made sense. Skully hadn't liked his brother much, and wasn't at all bothered by his death. But the motive... the motive had to be that Skully knew about the machine. Maybe it was a threat to him, or maybe he just wanted it for himself. Either way, that was motive for both murders, and with his criminal history, Skully made an excellent suspect.

Then I had an epiphany. I knew how Skully had found me at the tram station! He'd followed me there. Skully had tortured Gordy and then killed him right before I showed up, but hadn't found the plans inside the lab. Maybe I'd even interrupted his search. Skully and his goons had probably been waiting right across the street when I snuck out through that window, and called the cops on me to keep me from finding what they wanted. And I'd led them right to the blueprints at the depot. I snapped my fingers.

"What?" said Hank.

I blinked. For a second there, I'd forgotten that I was in mixed company. "Oh, nothing," I said. "Just disappointed that it doesn't work, that's all."

"Sure you are," he said. "Why are you smiling?"

I stared at him, weighing my options. Did I dare tell Hank Mossberg the truth, that I had solved both crimes? The first rule of business is that you never help the competition. You send them a Trojan horse now and then, but never something they can actually use...

A better question was: *What did I have to gain by telling him?* Well, it wasn't profit, that was for sure. There was no reward money. I'd never see a penny, and probably wouldn't even get any credit for solving the case, either.

On the other hand, he had me at a disadvantage. If I told the truth, it would clear my name instantly. That idea had a certain appeal, especially considering the fact that those handcuffs were getting uncomfortable. There were only two ways out of them, that I could think of. The second involved becoming an escaped convict, and that certainly wouldn't help my case at all. The last thing I wanted to do was to give the cops a legitimate reason to bust me. I sighed. It seemed I only really had one choice.

"All right," I said. "You two mooks listen up, 'cause I'm only gonna say this once. I know who the killer is, and I'm gonna tell ya everything..."

Chapter 12

And that's exactly what I did. I told them about sneaking out of the lab after finding Gordy's body, and about the word he'd whispered to me. I explained how Skully had followed me back to the depot after killing Gordy, and that was when we'd all been caught.

"So that's the whole story?" Hank said after I'd finished. He wore a skeptical look, as if somewhere in the back of that rock-like head of his he knew that I'd left a few things out.

"That's it," I said. "That's why Skully was at the depot. He followed me there, looking for that blueprint. Which only leaves two questions, if I'm right."

"And those would be?" Mickey chimed in cluelessly.

"A day late and a dollar short," I snorted. "The obvious questions are, A: Who told the cops I'd be there? And B: What does this machine do that makes it so important?"

They exchanged a glance. Between the two of them, they must've found two brain cells to rub together because at once, they both said: "We need to talk to Skully!"

"Well done," I said sarcastically. "So tell me boys, which one's the ventriloquist and which one's the dummy?"

"Shut it," Hank said.

"Just a joke, fellas. Hey, you think we could take off these cuffs now?"

"No," Hank said. "Not until I get a few questions answered. Let's move."

And just like that, we were off.

It took the better part of an hour to get back downtown because there had been a power outage and the trams were only running one way. That meant they had to circle the entire lake instead of moving back and forth between stops. As we made the long journey around the lake, I had plenty of opportunities to show off my shiny silver bracelets and hand out business cards.

Then, when we got downtown, we had to walk all the way from the tram stop to the precinct because Hank's too damned big to fit in a cab. That, and he's cheap. I mean, goblins can be cheap too, but at least we know when it's time to splurge. Hoofing it halfway across town isn't just tiring, it's also inefficient. But don't try explaining that to a daft-headed ogre.

It was six a.m. when we finally walked into the undercity police department. Hank stopped at the front desk and asked for one of the detectives, a wood-elf named Gen. Apparently, she was a friend of his. She was a looker, too. My eyes boggled when she stepped around the corner and told us to follow her back to her desk. Auburn hair, eyes like emeralds, curves that just wouldn't quit. She didn't have much going on personality-wise, sort of stiff and conservative for my tastes, like a librarian or a secretary... but you know what they say about the quiet ones.

I didn't even realize she was handicapped until we followed her back to her office, and I noticed a slight limp when she walked. As we settled down, I saw that she had a cane standing in the corner.

A FOOL THERE WAS

"I need to interview Skully Marcozi," Hank said without wasting a second on small talk.

"Marcozi?" Gen said with a frown. She glanced at me. "Hank, I thought you were here to turn in Snyvvle."

"You thought wrong," I blurted out. "I'm innocent, dame."

"Obviously," she said. "That's why you're wearing those handcuffs."

"Don't worry about Sam," Hank said. "I've got him under control. I need to see Marcozi immediately."

"I'm afraid that's not possible."

"Gen, I thought we had an agreement. Why is it that every time I need something, I have to put up a fight?"

She rolled her eyes. "Hank, it's not like that."

"Things must look different from that side of the desk. I suppose you have a reason for denying me access?"

"Yes, I do," she said in a cold tone. "Marcozi escaped three hours ago."

The room went silent. Gen looked at us, we looked at her.

"What happened?" Hank said at last. I could hear anger and impatience ruminating in his voice.

"To be honest, we're not sure. We had him under constant watch. We were going to let him cool in the cell for a while before questioning. When Chief Bossa got around to it, he went down there to bring Marcozi up and found the cell wide open and the guard lying unconscious on the floor."

"Are you kidding?" I said. "This is a police station for cripe's sake. How does someone escape from the police department?"

Hank and Gen exchanged a knowing glance. "You'd be surprised," Hank said. "It's not that hard."

"Very funny," said Gen. "At any rate, we issued a BOLO on him. Every cop in the city has his photo, so it won't be long before he's back in custody."

Hank sighed with a sound like the Hindenburg crashing. "Thanks anyway," he said, tipping his hat. "I'll be in touch."

We stepped out of Gen's office and headed for the exit. Halfway across the room, I heard a shout.

"MOSSBERG! What's going on here?" The entire office went quiet, and the cops around us tensed up.

We spun around to see the chief of police standing there, blinking his one big bloodshot eye. His name is Zane Bossa, and he's a cyclops. Zane's got a reputation as a real jerk. He's big, too. Not as big as Hank, but stocky, like a linebacker. Of course, his gut's even bigger than his chest, which doesn't do much for him, especially considering the guy's as ugly as a devil frog.

"Chief," Hank said with a nod, as calm as the eye of a tornado. "Was there something you needed?"

"Damn right there is!" he shouted. "Where do you think you're going with that prisoner?"

Hank narrowed his eyebrows. "Sam Snyvvle is *my* prisoner. He's my responsibility."

"Oh, no he's not!" the chief shouted. "That goblin is wanted in connection with two murders. I demand you release him into my custody!"

"No," Hank said flatly. He turned away and gestured for Mickey and me to follow. The chief turned bright red and came stomping in our direction.

"Arrest them!" he yelled at the top of his voice. "I want Hank Mossberg in chains!"

A FOOL THERE WAS

The cops all around us leapt out of their chairs and blinked uncertainly at each other. I think we all knew what was coming at that point, but nobody wanted to believe it was really happening. Personally, I'd rather step in front of a moving freight train than come between an ogre and an angry cyclops. I think everyone else felt that way, too. I took a step back and bumped into one of the cops. Neither of us moved.

When the chief realized nobody had jumped to follow his orders, he became enraged. He narrowed his great hideous eye, lowered his head, and broke into a run like a charging bison. The rest of us scrambled over each other to get out of the way. Hank didn't have time to react as the chief plowed into him at full speed. They went through a desk. When I say *through,* I mean that literally. Their combined weight absolutely destroyed that poor piece of furniture.

As they toppled over backwards, Hank somehow got the better of his opponent and regained his footing immediately. The chief pushed back to his feet. Hank threw his arms around the chief's midsection and lifted him into the air. I heard a scream as the cyclops' legs went flailing through the air. Hank lifted Zane over his head and tossed him backwards, onto the top of another desk. The coppers scrambled out of the way as he crashed down.

The chief lay there for a second on top of the wreckage, blinking up at the ceiling. For a second, I thought it was over. I was wrong.

Hank had just enough time to turn around and take three steps towards me before the chief leapt to his feet and launched into another attack. He tried rushing Hank a second time from behind, but this time the Steward was ready. Just as the chief was about to plow into him, Hank sidestepped the charge. Then, as the chief went hurtling by, Hank thrust out a hand and caught Zane by the collar. He gave it a good hard backwards yank. The chief's legs flew out from under him and suddenly, he was strangely horizontal in midair. Hank gave him a shove, slamming Chief Bossa down onto the floor. His breath went out with a loud *oomf!*

"Arrest him!" the chief choked. "Arrest them all!"

Hank knelt down, leaning over to look the chief in the eye. Then he decked the one-eyed tub of lard right in the face. The chief's eye rolled back in his head and fluttered shut. His body went still.

After that, the room got dead quiet. You could have heard a pin drop as Hank started for the exit. Mickey and I stared after him in awe, maybe a little fear. Hank paused by the front desk and glanced at us over his shoulder.

"You idiots coming, or not?"

Mickey and I jumped to hurry after him.

Nobody stopped us as we left the building. We were a block away before I realized that nobody was going to come after us.

"Holy crap," I said at last. "Mossberg, are you nuts? I've never seen anything like that." I glanced at Mickey. "Have you ever seen anything like that?"

Mickey ignored me. "What now, Boss?" he said to Hank.

We had reached the corner, and Hank stopped there, watching traffic fly up and down the boulevard.

"We have to find Skully," he said. "He has all the answers."

"How we gonna do that?" said Mickey. "He's probably a hundred miles away by now."

"Honey," I said matter-of-factly. They both looked at me.

A FOOL THERE WAS

"What?"

"Honey Love. Honey's the only other person who knew about the diamond. She's the one who hired me to find it in the first place."

"Now you tell us," Mickey groaned.

"What?" I said. "I gotta protect my clients."

"Is that what you call it?" Hank said stiffly.

"Whaddya mean?"

"Every person who knew about that diamond has been *murdered*, Sam. They even tried to kill *you*. I'll be shocked if Honey's even still alive."

I blinked.

"I hadn't thought of that," I said.

Outsmarted by an ogre. *Ouch*. It was a strange dose of humility, and I didn't like the taste of it at all. "She works at *The Lounge*," I said. "We've got to get over there!" I ran out into the street, whistling and waiving my cuffs in the air as I tried to hail a cab. For some reason, no one pulled up. I turned and shot Hank a glare.

"Would you get these things off me, please?"

Hank pursed his lips and looked me up and down. Then he gave Mickey a nod. The dwarf pulled a key out of his pocket and released me. I immediately went back to hailing cabs.

"Don't bother," Hank said. "I don't have any money."

"What?"

"I spent the last of it on our tram tickets downtown. We're going to have to walk."

I could only shake my head. "You're telling me the *Steward* can't afford a cab ride? What do they pay you, anyway?"

"Room and board," Mickey blurted. I laughed aloud. When I saw their dark looks, I reined it in.

"Sorry," I said. "I had no idea. Tell you what guys, the cab's on me."

Mickey's face lit up. Hank remained as stern and unreadable as ever. I waved my arms and whistled again, and this time a driver pulled up. The cabby was a middle-aged goblin wearing a *San Francisco Giants* baseball cap. He must not have seen Hank at first, because his eyes widened as the Steward stepped off the curb. Before he could protest, I pulled out my cash roll and waved it in front of him.

"We need to get to *The Lounge* in a hurry, bub," I said.

"Yes, sir!"

We climbed inside. Mickey and I shared the front. Hank squeezed sideways across the backseat. The cabby stomped on the pedal and I braced myself to take off like a rocket. The slug-like acceleration that followed was less than spectacular. I frowned as I leaned across Mickey and glanced at the speedometer.

"10 KPH," I muttered. "15... buddy, what's *wrong* with your car?"

"It's your pal in the backseat," he grumbled. "I should charge triple for what he weighs."

I hadn't thought of that. Then again, I was also used to my hotrod. I was pretty sure the size of the passenger wouldn't make much difference to my bored out 454 outfitted with a Holley four-barrel carb and a supercharger. I was running about seven hundred horses in my little Ford. That cab felt like it had about seventy. Cripes, I'd seen riding mowers move faster than that.

A FOOL THERE WAS

We finally made it across town in slightly less time than it would have taken to walk. We piled out of the cab and I paid the driver. I gave the guy a decent tip, not because he'd earned it, but because I knew I might need a ride in a hurry some cold and stormy night, and just my luck, he'd be the only guy around. *Think ahead!*

I also gave him my card. I get a lot of business from blue-collar guys like that cabby. When it comes down to it, the lower-middle income bracket is a P.I.'s number one moneymaker. The suburbs are filthy with cheating spouses, embezzling business partners, drug dealers, prostitutes, and blackmailers. It's the kind of stuff a soap opera writer would kill for, and it goes on all day long. A guy like me could make a lucrative living just handing out business cards in subdivisions all day long. I'm well enough established that most of my clients come to me, so I don't have to resort to that sort of behavior. Still, I never miss a chance to hand out my card. I consider it free advertising.

When we walked into *The Lounge,* I could sense a change in the place. It was early morning now, twilight time for the fae. The nocturnals had packed it in for the day; the diurnals were just getting out of bed. The crowd was mostly gone, and there was only one dancer on the stage. It wasn't Honey, though. It was a diva, a red-skinned offspring of a wood-nymph and a satyr. Her hair was lavender and the two small horns sprouting out of her forehead were gold. She was slow dancing on the pole for a crowd of five or six drunks, none of whom seemed to be paying much attention. Even the music had been turned way down.

Hank led the way up to the bar. The bartender was a goblin-kindred. He was human in physical proportions and coloration, but had the long ears and nose of a goblin. Like Pretty Boy, but not pretty. He was thin, wiry, and unshaven, and he had the dangerous glint in his eyes of a man who sells a lot more than just booze from behind the bar. The scar across his left eye spoke volumes about his job qualifications.

"Bar's closed," he said. "Come back this afternoon."

"I'm not here for a drink," Hank said. "I'm looking for Honey."

"And I said we're closed. Scram."

I saw Hank tensing up. Under normal circumstances, I would have loved to watch the ensuing fight, but unfortunately, I was in a hurry. I truly was worried about Honey's well-being.

"Never mind," I said. "I know where her dressing room is."

The bartender shot me a glare and I ignored him. I may have considered him a threat under different circumstances, but with Hank there, nobody could touch me.

I led the way around the stage to the entrance. The guard from the previous night wasn't even there. We stepped into the dark hallway behind the curtains and made our way back to Honey's room. I knocked on the door. When there wasn't an answer, I opened it.

"She's not here," Mickey said as we stepped inside. "We're too late."

"Everything's in place," Hank observed. "Looks like Honey didn't run into any trouble while she was here." He turned to me. "Why do I get the feeling that your girlfriend skipped town with that diamond?"

A FOOL THERE WAS

I considered that possibility for the thousandth time. I had my reasons to trust Honey, but I knew it wouldn't do any good to explain them to Hank. I'd just end up sounding like a love struck fanboy. Or worse yet, an easy mark. There's nothing worse for a goblin than being somebody's mark. It's the most humiliating thing that can happen to one of us. I'd rather be paraded down Bourbon Street naked in handcuffs than have somebody think I'd been used like a fool.

"She probably just went home," I said.

Mickey pulled a sheet of paper off the wall and handed it to Hank. It was Honey's work schedule. It also had her phone number and address printed on the bottom. Hank pulled out his smart phone. He tapped the screen with his huge green index finger, and the phone said, *"Speak now."*

"Dial five, five, twenty-two."

"Call Pizza Hut," the phone responded.

"No, dial five, five, twenty-two."

The phone ignored him. I could hear the faint sound of ringing on the other end of the line. Hank fumbled with the screen, trying to deactivate the call, but it made no difference.

"Cancel!" he ordered. "End call."

"Undercity Pizza Hut," a young male voice said.

"End call, dammit. HANG UP!"

"Excuse me?" said the pizza guy. "You called me, dude!"

"Sorry, wrong number," said Hank, holding the phone up to his mouth as if it were walkie-talkie. He tapped the screen a few more times and finally managed to hang up the call. Needless to say, by then I was rolling on the floor. Mickey glanced at me, slightly red in the face from trying not to bust out laughing. Hank angrily jammed the phone into his pocket and stormed into the hallway without a backwards glance. Mickey and I followed after him, shaking our heads.

When we exited the room, we took a left and headed back the way we had come. What we didn't notice was the security guard hiding in the shadows at the other end of the hall. As soon as we were out of the room, he shouted:

"On your knees! All of you!"

We all turned at once, and he took a step forward into the light. I had a sinking feeling as I recognized the guard I'd encountered there earlier. Hopefully, he'd forgotten about that.

"You!" he said, as soon as he saw me. "I should've known."

I grimaced. "Eh? You must be thinkin' of somebody else, bub."

"I don't think so. You're the guy who picked my pockets."

He jerked to the right and lifted what at first appeared to be a pistol. I was already ducking out of the way when I realized it was actually a stun gun. Not a bad model, either. Not as nice as mine, but not a cheapie like the ones they sell in the magazines.

He pulled the trigger and two probes shot out, whizzing right by my face at about ninety miles per hour. I crashed into the wall and glanced over my shoulder just in time to see Mickey light up like a Christmas tree. His body went rigid and his eyes got as big around as basketballs. Then he started to shake and I was pretty sure I could smell urine. I winced. I know exactly what that feels like.

The Steward was not amused by this turn of events. He let out a roar that shook the plaster off the walls. He charged the hobgoblin. The guard panicked as he saw the angry ogre bearing down on him, and turned to run. Too late, Hank

A FOOL THERE WAS

tackled the poor chump. They went down in a heap of flailing green limbs and cracking bones.

I took that as my cue, and quietly made my exit.

Chapter 13

I suppose it was sneaky of me, bailing on Hank at a time like that, especially considering it was my fault that the guard was so pissed in the first place. What can I say? I'm a goblin. Besides, Hank and his pet dwarf had been slowing me down all night. I was tired of it. I wanted to get back on the case, especially since I now knew that Hank and I were both at square one. I needed to get the jump on him, and when I saw the opportunity to do so, I acted. Meanwhile, Hank was back there wrestling in the dark with a hobgoblin. Maybe that's why I've got a house in the redwoods and Hank can't even afford cab fare.

Speaking of which, the first thing I did was hail a cab. I had seen her address back in the dressing room, and I told the cabby to get me there at the speed of light. He acquiesced, and didn't do a half-bad job of it. It helped that we didn't have a three-hundred pound ogre in the backseat.

Honey's place was down in the Old Quarter, at the southeastern end of the lake. As the name implies, it's one of the older parts of the city. As such, it tends to be low-income housing. It's not a bad neighborhood. The crime rate's low, unemployment is relatively low, and many of the families have lived in that neighborhood for a hundred years or more. The place is just old, and far enough out of the way that it's inconvenient. For the undercity, I guess you could call it rural.

Honey's street was too narrow and steep for a car, so the cabby dropped me off at the bottom of the hill and I climbed the rest of the way on foot. It wasn't a bad hike. I enjoyed the ambience of the neighborhood: the ancient, gnarled trees and vines, the uprooted cobblestones, the old brick buildings with wrought iron catwalks sprouting out of the upper levels. I felt like I'd stepped back in time.

Halfway up the hill, I came to Honey's address. It was a charming little house with a front porch and a balcony up above, all overgrown with ivy and honeysuckle. Even for the Old Quarter, I could tell the place wasn't cheap. Honey must have been doing fairly well for herself.

Of course she is, ya mook. You've seen her act.

As I climbed the steps, I heard the sound of voices drifting out of the front windows. I recognized Honey's voice, but not the man who was with her. He sounded big.

"I don't know what you were thinking," Honey said softly, sadly. "I really don't."

"I did it for you," he replied. "Can't you see that?"

"Of course... of course I do, Freddie. It's just that the timing is all wrong, that's all. It's not your fault."

"But it doesn't matter anymore. We can leave. We can take what we have and leave this place, and never come back!"

I heard a sniffle. It sounded like she was crying.

"What's the matter, baby?" he said. "Don't you know I love you?"

"Of course I do. That's the problem Freddie. Now you went and did something stupid. You're gonna get yourself killed."

A FOOL THERE WAS

I pursed my lips. They were talking in circles, but I could see where the conversation was headed. Honey was talking about splitting town. I had heard enough, so I pushed the door open and barged in. There they were, arms locked around each other, staring into each other's faces like two young lovers on the cover of a romance novel. Their jaws dropped as they saw me walk in. Mine dropped as I realized who Honey's lover was.

"Sam?" said Honey.

"Freddie the Fist?" I said in disbelief.

"Who do you think you are, buddy?" Freddie said.

Freddie disengaged from Honey's arms and took a step in my direction. He raised a fist the size of a cement truck and I winced because I knew I'd never get out of the way in time. *One hit, one kill.* That's what they'd put on my tombstone.

Honey caught him by the arm.

"Freddie, wait! It's okay, this is Sam. He's the private eye I hired."

Freddie looked me up and down. He lowered his fist. Then, to my surprise, extended his hand.

"Honey told me about how you were trying to help us. Thank you for that."

I shook his hand cautiously. At least a couple fingers, anyway. Freddie was even bigger than Hank. "Anything for a friend," I said. I glanced at Honey.

"I was so worried about you, Sam," she said.

"It looks like you got over it."

"Oh, stop that. I want you to meet my fiancé, Freddie."

"Pleased to make your acquaintance," I said politely. "I saw you fight at the *Palazio* the other night. Very impressive."

"Thanks," he said meekly. "It's the only thing I ever was any good at."

"I bet on the other guy. No offense, I hadn't heard of you. I'll know better next time."

"There won't be a next time," Honey said. "Freddie's fighting days are over."

I looked Freddie up and down. Somehow, he didn't seem as big as at first. Actually, that wasn't it. He looked worn out. He looked tired. I glanced at Honey.

"We have some things to talk about," I said.

"I know. We can talk in front of Freddie. He knows everything I do."

I took a deep breath. "All right. What happened to the diamond?"

"What do you mean?"

"Don't patronize me," I said angrily. "I heard you talking from outside. I know the two of you are up to something. You took that diamond, didn't you? You set me up to take the fall, so the two of you could take the money and run."

"No!" Freddie, said, pointing a finger at me. "You don't understand at all!" I flinched as he raised his hand. I realized I might have gotten a little carried away, so I adjusted my tone.

"Maybe somebody should explain it to me then," I said.

Honey settled onto the sofa, and Freddie joined her. She gestured for me to take the chair across from them. "Everything I told you was true," she said. "I hired you to steal the diamond from Pretty Boy, so Freddie and I could get married and start a family. We couldn't do that here. Not with… my past. We both wanted to move somewhere far away, to make a new start."

A FOOL THERE WAS

"Ireland," Freddie interjected. "Or Scotland, maybe. Someplace Pretty Boy and Skully couldn't track us down."

Good luck with that, I thought, but I decided it was best to keep my cynicism to myself. "Fair enough," I said. "But you lied to me. You said Pretty Boy had stolen that diamond from you. We both know that's not true."

Honey's eyes were downcast. "You're right. I lied to you, Sam. I hope you can forgive me for that. I honestly didn't think Pretty Boy would end up dead, though. That wasn't the plan at all. I just needed that diamond-"

"How'd you know about it?" I cut her off.

"I was Pretty Boy's mistress, for a while. Everything I told you about that is true. He showed it to me once. You must understand, Pretty Boy was cruel and violent. When he found out I had been seeing Freddie, he was furious. He said he was going to kill Freddie, and have me fired from my job. Then he changed his mind and told Freddie that he had to take a fall in the next fight. Since Freddie was the favorite, Pretty Boy would make a mint on the bets. Then he said he'd release Freddie from the contract."

I looked back and forth between the two of them, wondering how much of a chump I was for believing any of it. "All right," I said. "If all this is true, then who killed Pretty Boy?"

"It wasn't me, I swear it," Freddie blurted out. "He was already dead."

I raised an eyebrow. "Go on."

Freddie leaned forward, propping his elbows on his knees, and began wringing his hands. "I couldn't throw the fight. I just couldn't do it. I didn't want to take the fall. I didn't want to fight anymore, either, but I was willing to fulfill our contract. So I finished the fight. I won. Afterwards, I went to meet Pretty Boy to talk him out of our agreement. I knew he'd be angry about the fight, but I figured if I caught him at home alone, he wouldn't kill me. So I went in through the secret passage..."

"Passage?" I echoed, my eyes widening. "How'd you know about it?"

He averted his gaze. "Pretty Boy and I... we had a *thing* going for a while."

My eyebrows went even higher. They probably touched together at the top of my head. So the rumors about Pretty Boy's thing for young hobgoblins was true. Not only that, but apparently he'd been in a relationship with Honey and Freddie at the same time. I suddenly found the rabbit hole getting quite deep. Too deep, and in the wrong direction...

"When I found him, he was already dead," Freddie said quickly.

"So if it wasn't you who shot him, then who?"

Freddie frowned, creating deep marks across his massive green hobgoblin forehead. "Nobody shot him. What are you talking about?"

"What are you talking about?"

"Pretty Boy, obviously. When I found him, he was dead in his chair. He was foaming at the mouth, like he'd been poisoned."

"No," I said, making a sweeping gesture. "Pretty Boy was shot, right through the chest. I saw the body myself. There was a hole the size of your fist right through him."

"Not when I was there," Freddie said adamantly. "I'm telling you, Pretty Boy was poisoned."

A FOOL THERE WAS

"Cripes." I rose to my feet and began pacing back and forth. I was trying to sort it all out in my head; trying to marry the facts of the murder with the suspects and the new information I had. I started mumbling:

"If what you say is true, then somebody else was in that room before you were there, and somebody *else* after you left. If Pretty Boy was really dead when you got there, then whoever was first, that's the real murderer... but then after you left, a third party came along and shot him. Why would someone do that? Why would someone shoot a man who's already dead?"

Freddie looked at me with his hands spread wide in a gesture of complete puzzlement. It was a fitting look for a hobgoblin. That was probably what he looked like every time he opened a book, or watched Final Jeopardy, or tried to read an instruction manual...

Suspects, I thought. *Honey and Freddie. Skully Marcozi. Pretty Boy's ex-wife, Sheba. Nyva perhaps, although she claimed to have been out of the country... Who else?*

"Three people were in that room the night Pretty Boy was murdered," I continued. "The killer, followed by you Freddie, and then the shooter... The safe!" I said, snapping my fingers. "Was the safe open when you got there?"

Freddie hung his head. "Yeah, that's how I got this." He reached into his pocket and withdrew a paper. He handed it to me and I looked it over.

"Your contract?"

"Of course," Honey said. "When Freddie found Pretty Boy dead, he knew he had the chance to destroy the contract without anybody finding out. And why wouldn't he? The safe was wide open. All he had to do was reach in and take it, and then sneak back out of there."

I looked at him. "Is all of this true?"

"Of course. I just wanted my freedom, that's all."

"And what about the diamond?"

"I can't tell you anything about it, except that I was tempted when I saw it in the safe, and all that money in there, but I didn't take it. That would be wrong, and stealing back my contract was bad enough already-"

"Hold it! You're telling me the Scarlet Tear was *in the safe* when you were there?"

"Sure," he said. He glanced at Honey. "See, this is *why* I didn't take it. We would have been caught already."

She rolled her eyes and sighed. "We would have already been in Fiji, lover. Now look at us."

"I have some thinking to do," I said, reaching for the door. "I'd advise the two of you to lay low."

"We'll stay right here until we hear from you," Honey promised.

"No, Skully knows about the two of you. He probably believes you have the diamond. It's not safe here. Call a cab. Go find a cheap motel and don't let anybody know where you are."

"How will we know when it's safe?"

"Watch the news," I said, straightening my hat. "When this is all over, everyone will know."

I stepped outside and started down the stairs. I made it three steps before I realized Honey had followed me. I turned to stare at her curiously, as she quietly closed the door behind us. She fixed me with a watery gaze.

A FOOL THERE WAS

"I'm sorry, Sam. I really am. I didn't mean to hurt you, leading you on like I did."

"Don't be ridiculous," I said.

"Don't blame Freddie. I didn't mean to fall in love with him, but I just couldn't help myself. I want to be with him forever. I want to have his children. Can you forgive me?"

I looked her up and down. "I can't, because it didn't mean anything. We both knew that. It didn't mean anything, that's all."

"Okay, Sam."

She went back inside, and I found myself alone in the cool, still night.

I took a deep breath. Deep down, I knew better than to think I could ever have anything real with a girl like Honey. A guy like me? Not a chance. Nothing more than a one night stand, anyway. It did get under my skin though, the fact that she'd kept her relationship with Freddie secret from me. When it came down to it, she'd been using me all along. Which wasn't super surprising, but it was disappointing.

It didn't matter, I thought. It was just a game. She had played her part and I'd played mine. We had done it before, and we would again. Regardless, I hoped Honey and Freddie would take my advice about laying low. I would have hated to see something terrible happen to them. Seeing as how everybody else connected to that diamond had been killed, it was only a matter of time until the killers came for Honey. They had even come gunning for me, and I'd never even seen that rock.

That's the joy of being a private eye, I suppose. It's like walking around with a target painted on your back. Half the people you meet want to kill you, the other half want to use you. All I really care about is when I get to cash the paycheck.

Which was a concern that had been growing in the back of my mind all day long. If Honey didn't have that diamond, and would probably never get it, then who the hell was going to *pay my fee?* I had half a mind to drop the whole case. Unfortunately, the bad guys weren't just gunning for Honey and Freddie. They were gunning for me, too. I was in it up to my neck, and I sure as heck wasn't going to hand everything over to Hank Mossberg hoping he'd eventually stumble onto the truth. Even if he did, by then it would probably be too late for me. In the interest of self-preservation, I didn't have much choice. I *had to* see the case through to the end. If I didn't, I was going to end up just like Gordy and Pretty Boy, and that's just bad business.

It was after eight a.m. when I finally caught a cab. It was getting late and I had half a mind to go home and get some rest, but that wasn't really an option. Hank Mossberg knew about my place in the woods. If he knew, I might as well assume it was common knowledge. I was tempted to take my own advice and go find a cheap hotel, but then I had another idea. It occurred to me that only one person out there really had the answers I was looking for, and that was Skully. Unfortunately, Skully was on the run and there was no way to know where he'd turn up next.

But that wasn't true, was it? I had just warned Honey that he would probably be looking for her. It was only a matter of time until he showed up at her place... I told the cabby to turn around.

Five minutes later, I was walking back up the street. I stuck to the left side, where the shadows were a little deeper. I had my

A FOOL THERE WAS

eye on an alley up ahead, where I might be able to see whoever came and went...

"I had a feeling you'd show up here," said a deep growly voice.

I cringed. Then I took off like a bat out of hell. I made it as far as the next alley, and that was when Mickey jumped out of the shadows and beaned me upside the head with a broken two-by-four. I saw stars, and felt my brain rattling around inside my head like a pinball machine.

Next thing I knew, I was on my back staring up at the fog as it drifted over the rooftops. I heard movement, and saw Hank's face appear above me. Mickey's face appeared too, grinning like a piglet at a trough.

"Where you going in such a hurry?" Mickey said. "Come to finish off the last witness?"

I groaned.

"Get him up," said Hank. "We've got movement."

Mickey tossed the board aside. He grabbed me by the shoulders and jerked me to my feet. Then he dragged me back into the shadows of the alley. He leaned in close and whispered, "Keep your mouth shut."

I turned my head dizzily towards the mouth of the alley. Hank loomed in front of us, blocking the view of the street. I tried to take a step closer to see if I could peek around him and see what was going on, but Mickey yanked me back and shoved me up against the wall. The silly little dwarf actually looked like he might get violent. I never knew he had it in him.

I almost reached for my ring, but then decided against it. I knew I could take Mickey out in a heartbeat, but Mossberg was another story. There was no way out of that alley except around him, and I knew Hank wouldn't take kindly to me putting his deputy in the hospital.

"It's Honey," Hank whispered after a few seconds. "She's packed her bags. She's leaving with somebody... a big hobgoblin."

"Freddie the fist," I said. Hank looked at me questioningly. I quickly explained everything.

"You don't have to worry about Honey," I said. "She's just keeping out of sight until things are safe."

"We're not here for her anyway," said Mickey. "It's Skully we're looking for."

"Yeah?" I said with a smile. I saw a dark look pass between them and Mickey gulped as he realized he'd said more than Hank wanted him to. "Easy fellas, we're playing for the same team."

"No, we're not," said Hank. "You're playing for nobody but Sam."

"Oh? And whose side are you on, exactly? Truth, justice, and the American way? Really, Hank? 'Cause the last time I checked, you were a fugitive, too."

I could tell from the look in his eyes that Hank didn't like being reminded that after his altercation at the precinct, he was now on the wrong side of the law. "Don't push your luck," he grumbled. "I might just change my mind."

I frowned, trying to work out what he meant by that statement. It didn't take much figuring to realize what Hank was implying. If he wanted to get back in the chief's good graces, all Hank really had to do was turn me in. I hadn't even considered that possibility. He wouldn't do that, though. Not

A FOOL THERE WAS

this close to catching Skully. Not when all we had to do was wait...

"Cool down," I said, trying to sound convincing. "All I meant was that I'm here for the same reason as you. I knew Honey was bait, but I didn't want her getting hurt. That's why I gave you the slip, so I could warn her. No harm done. Skully won't even know until it's too late. When he comes around, we'll grab him. That simple."

"Why should we trust you?" said Mickey. "You already escaped once."

"To *warn* her," I said. "I already told you, I didn't want Honey to get caught in the crossfire. Besides, I want Skully behind bars as much as you."

"Why's that?"

"Because he's the only proof that I didn't do any of this. He's the killer, not me. Plus, as long as he's on the streets, I'm as good as dead."

Hank looked at me skeptically. "We'll see," was all he said.

"Look, Skully's already tried to kill me twice. He had two goons try to shoot me up in a parking garage. Then he planted a bomb in my house. I'm lucky to still be alive. I won't breathe easy until he's locked up for good. That's the honest truth."

"Good," Hank said with a smile. "At least there's some justice in this world."

I didn't care much for the way he said that, or the implication behind it, but I let it go. "Can I at least sit down?" I said. "Your partner almost brained me. My skull is splitting."

Hank nodded towards the back of the alley, and told Mickey to keep an eye on me. As we wandered back into the shadows, Hank remained to hover at the corner, watching the street. I settled down on a stack of old pallets across from a rusty old dumpster, and leaned up against the brick wall. The cool bricks felt good against my head, and the stinky, mildewy air reminded me of my youth. I breathed in the musty scent and smiled as my thoughts drifted back to the days of glory and adventure and really good food.

Chapter 14

The dream didn't last long. I sensed a presence next to me and my eyes snapped open. It was Hank. He was standing over me with a finger to his lips, warning me to keep quiet. I nodded that I understood, and rose to my feet.

We quietly moved up to the mouth of the alley. Hank gestured for me to look up the street. He stepped aside so I could take a peek. I put my face up to the corner of the building, and very slowly moved my head out.

It was dark now... or *darker*, I should say, since dark is a relative term in the undercity. The difference is that during the daytime, shafts of sunlight shine down through holes in the ceiling of the cavern. At night, some parts of the undercity are pitch black. It must have been close to six p.m., I realized. I'd slept on those crates all day long. It had only seemed like a few minutes.

I peered up the darkened street and saw the shape of a man standing on Honey's front porch. A goblin, actually. It was Skully, dressed in a long white leather trench coat. He was accompanied by a hobgoblin, and I could make out several more shadowy figures moving in the darkness around the house. I estimated six, maybe seven in total. I pulled my head back into the alley and fixed my gaze on Hank.

"Too many," I whispered.

He motioned for me to step back and he peered around the corner.

"How many, exactly?" he whispered.

I'd forgotten about Hank's humanlike vision. Ogres can't see very good in the dark, and neither can dwarves. I had to grin, because I knew what power I held over them. If I wanted to, I could have sent them right up to that door. That would have been the end of my Hank Mossberg problem. Unfortunately, I'd still be stuck with my Skully problem, and that was even worse.

"Don't jerk me around," Hank said, sensing my thoughts.

"Seven."

"We have to assume they're armed," he whispered.

I nodded. "They usually are."

Hank fixed me with a serious gaze. "Sam, I need your help."

"Forget it, bub. I'm not getting shot for nobody."

"That's not it. I need you to call the cops."

"What are you talking about?"

"There's no cell service this far out. I need you to run back down the hill and call Gen. She's in my address book." Hank handed me his phone. I accepted it with a bewildered look. "I'm trusting you with our lives, Sam," he added seriously.

I stared at the phone, a feeling of guilt and self-loathing gnawing at my gut. Why would he do that? Hank knew he couldn't trust me. I'd already split on him once. What would keep me from doing it again? I looked up into his face and then glanced at Mickey. Suddenly I felt sick to my stomach.

"I don't know, maybe the kid should do it," I said reluctantly.

A FOOL THERE WAS

"No," Hank said. "He can't move in the darkness like you. The second we walk out of this alley, Mickey and I will be moving targets. You're the only one who can get down the hill without them seeing you." He placed his hand on my shoulder. "You can do it, Sam. *I trust you.*"

"Don't make me gag," I said. I felt my energy ebb towards his hand and quickly pulled away. "Next you'll want to hug me or something."

Hank grinned. "Get moving."

He could see right through me. I hated that. I felt like a kid caught stealing from the cookie jar. I suddenly wanted to get out of that alley just so he wouldn't be looking at me anymore.

I glanced around and decided that the street was the worst possible way out of there. Instead, I latched onto an aluminum rain gutter that ran down the length of the wall and started to climb.

I could feel Hank and Mickey's eyes on me as I scurried up the side of the building. They couldn't have made that climb in a million years, but for me it was child's play. I was light enough that the gutter hardly even noticed my weight. My shoe tips easily found and slipped into the tiny ledges on the corners of the bricks. Up I went, like a squirrel climbing a tree. Ten seconds later, I was over the ledge and out of sight.

Up on the roof, I paused to check Hank's cell phone for reception. It still had no signal. I glanced back up the hill and realized I had an almost perfect vantage of Honey's house. I saw Skully on the front porch, and his companions sneaking around the back. I recognized the long slim shapes of tommy guns and batons in their hands. I heard a "*psst*" sound and glanced down over the ledge of the roof.

"Move it!" Hank whispered loudly, waving me away. I rolled my eyes at him and took off.

Hank had been right, of course. Getting out of that alley and down the hill wasn't a challenge for me at all, but him or Mickey never would have made it. That didn't make me feel any better about the fact that I was playing the unfamiliar role of a reluctant hero. I don't like being a chump. No goblin does. And it doesn't get any chumpier than saving the guy you've considered an enemy for as long as you've known him. I felt like an absolute schmuck.

When I got down to the main road, I dialed up Gen's number. She didn't know it was me, so she answered right away. Then of course, I had to explain everything. She wanted to know how I'd gotten Hank's phone and what I had done to him… in other words, all the usual accusations. I told her not to worry her pretty head about it and that if she ever wanted to see Hank alive again, she'd better get rolling and bring a swat team with her. Then I hung up on her.

Suddenly I felt better about things. Sure, I may have made myself sound like the villain instead of the hero, but at least I wasn't a chump. I smiled as I started back up the hill. Soon everyone would know that I had been singlehandedly responsible for the capture of a serial murderer and the rescue of the Steward himself. That's the kind of publicity money just can't buy. Maybe they'd even have to give me a medal…

I climbed back on the roof and made my way back to the ledge overlooking the house. I saw that Skully and his boys had busted down the doors, and they were frantically searching inside the house for Honey. The lights were on, and I could see their silhouetted shapes in the windows as they went upstairs

A FOOL THERE WAS

to search the bedroom, and then down into the basement. It was at that point that I realized we had a problem.

I had only hung up with Gen a few minutes earlier. I knew it would be at least ten more minutes before the cavalry showed up. By then it would be too late. Skully would be gone, and the cops would show up to find the three of us looking as guilty and stupid as mountain trolls. I had to do something. I had to find a way to slow them down...

Hank must have come to the same conclusion, because I heard a rustling noise and looked down just in time to see him walk out of the alley and up the street. My jaw dropped open. I shot Mickey a worried look and he spread his arms as if to say, "I know, but who can stop him?"

You got a death wish? I thought, looking at Hank.

I made a "psst" sound and waved my arms, trying to get the Steward's attention, trying to call him back, but he ignored me. He moved right out into the middle of the street as if to make sure they'd see him, and then marched straight up to the house.

It didn't take long.

"Mossberg?" I heard Skully's voice echoing back and forth between the buildings.

"Don't make this any harder than it has to be," Hank said. "I'm taking you all in."

"Ha! You and what army?" As he spoke, I saw Skully's companions come out of the house and spread out around him. They raised their guns, and trained their sights on Hank.

"You don't want to do that," Hank said.

"Why not?" said Skully.

"First, because you're surrounded by witnesses. The people in all these houses might be afraid of you, but when they see what you've done, they'll come forward. This is one murder rap you won't walk away from. Second, I don't like getting shot. *It pisses me off.*"

Skully faltered when Hank said that. He'd heard the rumors, too. There are all kinds of stories about Hank's exploits. Stories about him getting shot, about bullets that hadn't even penetrated his skin. Stories about him taking out an entire gang of *Greenbloods* singlehandedly, and coming out without a scratch. Until now, I'd chalked all that up to urban legends. Nobody could survive all that. Suddenly I wasn't so sure. Neither was Skully.

"I like you, Mossberg," he said. "You've got more guts than my entire crew put together. Guts won't save you, though. Not from four machine guns. On the other hand, I can save you."

"How are you gonna do that?" Hank said defiantly.

"I'm going to give you a choice. Either you walk out of here quietly and pretend this never happened, or you accept my offer and never look back."

"What offer might that be?"

"Work for me. I can pay you more money than you've ever dreamed about, much less seen. I can give you money, women, prestige... you name it, it's in my power. Think about it: *Hank Mossberg, the terror of the underworld.* The monster that monsters have nightmares about. That could be you, Steward. It's all there for the taking."

Hank was silent for a moment, and then suddenly broke out laughing. "I expected more imagination from someone like you."

A FOOL THERE WAS

"Don't be a fool," Skully said angrily. "There's only one choice left. You don't want that one. There's no glory in a six-foot hole, Steward."

"Maybe not, but there is the satisfaction that you won't be far behind."

Skully made a gesture and two of his men came forward, brandishing their weapons. I heard a noise and glanced back down the hill towards the main road. I saw at least two dozen cops in black swat gear hustling up the hill. Some of them were armed with semi-automatic rifles. That was comforting, but I knew it wouldn't make any difference. They couldn't get to the house before Skully's goons filled Hank full of holes.

I stood up, waving both arms in the air.

"Skully!" I shouted at the top of my lungs. "Skully, I see you!"

Skully and his men paused with their fingers on the triggers. Hank swerved his head in my direction.

"Who is that?" Skully said cautiously.

I laughed as loud as I could. "What? You don't remember me? I'm hurt!"

"Is that Snyvvle?" he shouted. "Sam Snyvvle?"

"You got me Skully! And I've got something you want!" I pulled the paper out of my pocket and unfolded it. I knew he wouldn't recognize it at that distance, but it didn't matter. "It's the blueprint for Pretty Boy's machine. Isn't this what you wanted?"

Skully looked at two of his men and jerked his head in my direction. "Bring him down here," he mumbled. They took off in my direction. They made it halfway to the alley before the swat team pounced from the shadows.

Both goblins cried out as the cops took them to the ground, and the noise got Skully's complete attention. He took a step forward at the same moment that a small metal cylinder landed on the front lawn. It exploded with the light of a thousand suns. Or so it seemed to this goblin, anyway. There was a crack like thunder and another flash of lightning, but by then it was all just a haze to me. My nightvision had been fully active when that first flash-bang grenade went off, and it blinded me completely.

A wave of disorientation washed over me. I heard sounds of shouting and fighting echoing all around me. I turned and tripped over something. It turned out to be the edge of the roof. Next thing I knew, I was falling head over heels off the side of the building. I landed with a backbreaking crash in the alley below, and a supernova went off inside my head. After that, I was off to lala land for a few hours.

I woke up in Fairy General with a splitting headache and an I.V. tube stuck in my arm. A nurse who looked like Salma Hayek with pointy ears and silver-streaked hair was looking over my chart. She wrote something down, and replaced the board on the hook by the door.

"How are you feeling, Mister Snyvvle?" she said.

"Like roadkill."

"It's a wonder you're alive. You took quite a blow to the head. You have a concussion." She bent over me and I couldn't help noticing the way the fabric of her uniform parted at that last button. She touched my head and I let out a yelp.

"Cripes! Warn a guy before you do that!"

A FOOL THERE WAS

"Sorry, just checking. You have quite a nasty bruise."

"Why don't you kiss it for me and make it better?"

"I suppose I could, but then what would you learn from all of this?"

"If you think there's a lesson to be learned here, you're going about it all wrong," I said. "Life ain't about learning a lesson, it's about winning."

She stood back and stared at me. "And how does one *win* life?"

"By not losing."

"That's quite a philosophy. Unfortunately, you're a little short on word count if you want to make it into a bestseller."

"No sweat, I'll sell it to Hollywood. By the time they're done with the idea, it'll be three movies and a prequel."

She snorted. "Very funny. You seem to be feeling all right."

"Sure, dollface. What've you got in mind?"

She opened the door and stuck her head out. "You can see him now."

My eyebrows went up as the nurse stepped aside and Mickey walked in, grinning like a kid with a lollipop. He was followed by Gen, and the big guy...

"Hank?" I said. "What are you guys doing here?"

"You didn't think we'd leave you here all alone, did you?" said Mickey.

"Not after that stunt you pulled on the roof," said Gen. "You nearly got yourself killed."

"And you saved my life," Hank said. "I owe you for that, Sam."

"Stop it before I puke," I said, waving him off. "You're just trying to weasel in on my reward."

"Ah," said Gen. "About that. I'm afraid there is no reward. We only lost custody of Skully for a few hours, and the chief-"

"Whatever. Just tell me you caught him this time."

"We did. He's in custody right now, thanks to you," Gen said proudly. "And the chief has agreed to drop all charges against you, for now at least."

"Wait a minute," I said, eyeing her up and down. "What do you mean he's *in custody?* You guys had him in custody *the last time* he escaped."

"He's not in police custody," Mickey said. "The Elders have him."

"Elders?"

"Yep. They're taking over the case. It was either that or let Hank and the chief go head to head. Nobody wanted to see how that might turn out."

I considered that. The Elders are sort of the supreme law among the fae. They're super powerful and -supposedly- wise wizards. One might say they're the rulers of our government, although we don't technically have such a thing. They *are* powerful though, I know that much for a fact. I just also happen to believe that wherever there's a super-powerful wizard, there's also a midget behind a curtain.

"The Elders will convene tomorrow for a hearing," Hank said. "You're invited to testify, of course. If you think you can make it, that is."

"Of course I can," I said. I glanced around the room. "Where are my clothes?"

"I'll get them for you," said Gen. She walked over to the closet and pulled out a large plastic bag with all my belongings. I shot Hank a look.

A FOOL THERE WAS

"Why don't you and the kid go for a walk while Gen gets me dressed?" I said with a smirk.

"Very funny," said Gen. She threw the bag at me. "Get yourself dressed, and hurry up. Lunch is on the police department."

"Well it isn't a sponge bath, but I'll take it."

Lunch was a strange event. Looking back over the whole scene, I can't help thinking it was more like something out of a movie than real life. Then again, life in the undercity always has a dramatic flair. How could it not? A thousand different species of creatures, each with its own culture and politics... it's like a microcosm of the entire world, with a healthy dose of magic tossed in just to throw everything off. There's never a dull moment in the undercity. I suppose that's why I'd never want to live anywhere else.

Considering our history, sitting at that table with those three coppers should've been the most uncomfortable thing I had ever done. Strangely, it wasn't. We placed our orders, and while we waited, Mickey recounted what it was like watching me standing on that roof, shouting at the top of my lungs, and then taking a swan dive into the alley. We all laughed about that. Then we talked about Hank's seemingly suicidal march up to the house, and his confrontation with Skully.

We had some good laughs. I was surprised when Hank began to complain about all the work he had on his plate. I'd always thought he loved being the Steward, but from the sound of things, it was more of a burden than anything. He said most of the time people came to him complaining about a rude clerk at the checkout counter or a dispute with the power company.

"At least you're busy," I said, hinting at the fact that he had stolen a large portion of my business.

"Too busy," Mickey said. "And after all the work we do, half the time people don't even pay us."

"That's why I keep Mickey on the payroll," said Hank.

"Oh? So he does all the leg-breaking?" I joked.

"No," Mickey laughed. "But I'm great at guilt trips. I give them the old puppy dog eyes and they don't know what to think." To prove his point, he stuck out his lower lip and grimaced like he'd been stabbed with a hot poker.

"I believe that," I said. A dwarf without a beard is creepy enough. When he made that face, I wanted to reach across the table and slap him.

Gen got a phone call while we were waiting for the bill. She hung up with a glowing smile on her face.

"Good news?" said Hank.

"I think we got another break. The lab results came back on that glass. Pretty Boy's orange juice was laced with aspartame." Hank got a grave look.

"What the hell is that?" I said.

"It's an artificial sweetener used by humans," he said. "For them, it's generally regarded as harmless, but for the fae, it's lethal."

"You should see what happens when people feed it to fairies," Mickey added. "Their blood is already seventy percent sugar. That's why they smell like cotton candy. They have a hyper metabolic rate, and when they eat fake sugar, *poof!*... It's not pretty."

"Fae blood and aspartame don't mix, period." Gen said. "The more fae blood a kindred has, the faster it'll kill him."

A FOOL THERE WAS

"That explains the foaming at the mouth," I mumbled. They all looked at me.

"What are you talking about?" said Hank.

Oops. I'd forgotten that I hadn't shared that bit of information with him. There was no backtracking now. "I suppose it can't hurt to tell ya," I said. "Freddie the Fist saw Pretty Boy right after he died. Said he was foaming at the mouth like he'd been poisoned."

"And you were going to tell us this when?" said Gen.

"Wait a minute," Hank said. "What does Freddie the Fist have to do with this?"

"He was, uh... well, you've heard the rumors, right?" They all looked at me expectantly. I grimaced. "Pretty Boy had a... he had a thing for *big boys*. Mostly hobgoblins."

"You mean Freddie was his-" said Mickey, but Hank interrupted him.

"We get it," he said. "Thing is, I'd heard Pretty Boy had a thing going on with Honey Love."

"He did," I said. "Pretty boy had lots of things going on."

"I guess so," said Gen. "How does this affect our case, Hank? Does this mean Freddie is a suspect now, too?"

Hank gave me an expectant look. "Well?"

"No. Freddie and Honey were all wrapped up with Pretty Boy, but they wanted out. When Freddie found the body, he saw the safe open and took his contract. He left everything else in there."

"You sure about that?" said Hank.

"Yes, because I got there after him and everything was there except for the diamond. The thing was full of cash and gold."

"So maybe Freddie took the diamond," said Mickey.

I shook my head. "If Freddie had the diamond, he'd be long gone. There was no reason for him and Honey to stick around this long. Besides, Freddie said that when he got there, Pretty Boy hadn't been shot. He didn't even know about it."

"Then someone else was there," said Hank. "Someone after him, but before you?"

"I'd bet my toenails on it."

"Keep your toenails," said Gen. She looked at Hank. "Where does that leave us?"

"Sheba. Everything keeps leading back to her."

"I already talked to her," I said. "She wanted Pretty Boy dead, but she didn't do it."

"And you trust her?" said Hank. "Why is that?"

I smiled meekly. "Because Sheba thought *I had* killed Pretty Boy."

Hank looked askance at me, as if he were trying to figure out my motive in all this.

"Oh, stop before you hurt yourself," I said. "I allowed Sheba to believe I had killed her ex, because she was spewing information like a deep sea oil rig. She was throwing a party over it, for cripe's sake."

Hank considered that for a minute. I could tell he wasn't satisfied.

"I want to talk to her again," he said. "Something's missing here. Mickey, call Tas and have him run Sheba's financial records. See if there's a charge on her credit cards at a grocery store topside."

"For aspartame?" Mickey said.

"Exactly. If she did buy it, hopefully she was dumb enough to leave a paper trail. Also check up on Nyva Marcozi's alibi. I

A FOOL THERE WAS

want proof she was in the Alps, and not back home, poisoning her husband." He rose from the table and looked at Gen.

"I can't go with you," she said. "I've got enough trouble with the chief right now. Call me if you learn anything."

"Will do." Hank looked me up and down. "Well, you coming or not?"

"Of course I'm coming," I said. "I've got way too much riding on this case to leave it in the hands of an amateur like you."

I think he actually smiled. Either that, or he was fighting the urge to eat me.

Chapter 15

Gen and Mickey both went on their way. Mickey had work to do back at the office and Gen needed to keep up appearances with her boss, so for the rest of the day it was just the two of us. Hank and I took a cab to The Wall, paid for -of course- by yours truly. We ran into Wyllem, the young elevator attendant. He recognized me from my previous visit, and greeted us with a smile.

"Any word?" I said, referring to our agreement.

"No, sir! Mrs. Barsto has been holed up in her flat for two solid days with her sister. She finally ended the party yesterday. She threw everybody out in a drunken rage. Since then, it has been quiet."

"Thanks, bub." I handed him another fifty and ignored Hank's scowl of disapproval. We stepped into the elevator. The doors closed, and I was alone with the Steward. He was still scowling.

"Ah, lay off," I said. "You got a problem with the way I do business?"

He ignored me.

"At least I get results," I said. And then it clicked. I turned to stare up into his face, and saw the glimmer of resentment in his eyes. "That's it, isn't it? You hate the fact that I get results this way."

"It's a free city," he grunted.

"Ain't nothing free in the undercity. Maybe if you understood that, you wouldn't always be a step behind m-"

Hank caught me by the throat and lifted me up, pushing me against the wall. I struggled, kicking at him as the energy started to drain out of me. I choked, gasping for breath. The world started to go dark.

Without a word, Hank let me drop. I crashed to the floor and sat there, rubbing the ache out of my neck. It had all happened in three seconds.

"What was that for?" I said angrily.

"You talk too much."

I pushed to my feet and stared at him. I took a couple steps to the side, giving him room. The next time he reached for me, I'd be ready.

It never came to that, though. The elevator *dinged* and the doors opened. Hank and I stepped into the hallway. He knocked on Sheba's door. A few seconds later, she was there.

"Steward!" she said pleasantly. "What a surprise to see you back here!"

I couldn't help but notice that she was using the same flirtatious tone with Hank that she had used with me. I wasn't surprised. She was a woman, and for all I knew, possibly a killer. But I repeat myself.

I stepped out from Hank's shadow.

"What about me, dollface? Am I a surprise, too?"

Sheba's eyes widened as she saw me. For a moment, she actually went speechless. She looked at Hank, and then back at me… "Well," she stammered. "How about that? I never expected the two of you to show up here together."

A FOOL THERE WAS

"I bet you didn't," I said, pushing past her into the apartment. "I think I'm starting to get the picture now."

Hank followed me in and she closed the door behind us. "Gentlemen, I wasn't expecting company. Can... can I get you something to drink?"

"No thanks," said Hank. "I just have a few questions for you."

She gestured towards the couch. Hank followed her into the living room. I stood back, watching her hips sway, watching the long auburn strands of hair part around her small pointy dryad-elf ears, admiring the way the short, skin-tight dress she wore clung to her curves. She was a liar, but that didn't mean I couldn't look.

Just as she was about to sit, I said:

"I'll help myself to that drink."

I headed for the kitchen. Sheba moved to stop me, but then realized she couldn't leave Hank alone in the living room. She didn't want either one of us wandering through her apartment alone, and I was pretty sure I knew why. Unfortunately, it was going to happen one way or another. She slumped her shoulders as she realized it was hopeless. I disappeared through the doorway with a smile on my face. I instantly started tearing the place apart.

I went through the pantry first, pushing aside all the boxes of pasta and bags of sugar (fae creatures thrive on sugar) and then I rummaged through the cabinets over the stove. I searched every drawer and cabinet and came up with nothing. Then something occurred to me. I yanked open the side-by-side fridge and started to scan its contents. No surprises there, either. Cola, ice cream, sugary treats galore... and then I found it. The aspartame was in a liquid form, in a small plastic bottle on the top shelf in the door. I turned it over in my hands.

It was a clearly labeled commercial product, right out of a human grocery store. The instructions said to use half a teaspoon of aspartame to replace two teaspoons of sugar. What it neglected to say was: *Kills Fairies on Contact!* I stared at the clear liquid, wondering how such a simple thing could be so potent. It may as well have been a bottle of arsenic. I closed the fridge and wandered out into the living room.

The second I appeared, Sheba jerked her head around and fixed her gaze on the bottle in my hand. I held it up so Hank could see it, and his face darkened. She was sitting in the chair across from him, and she immediately dropped her head into her hands and began to sob.

"It's time to come clean," Hank said.

"I'm sorry," she said, the sound of her voice muffled through her hands. "I didn't mean for all this to happen."

"You mean you didn't plan to get caught," I said cynically.

"No, that's not it at all. You don't understand."

"Walk us through it," said Hank. "Start at the beginning." He handed her a tissue, and she dabbed at her eyes.

"All right… It all started a few months ago. It was a Saturday night, and my sister had been out dancing with Pretty Boy. It was cold and stormy, and Nyva showed up here drenched to the bone. She had a black eye, and bruises on her arms. I knew it was him. I knew it immediately, because he used to do the same things to me."

"He'd been beating on her," said Hank.

"Thanks, Captain Obvious," I said, rolling my eyes. "Let the lady talk, would you?"

A FOOL THERE WAS

Hank ignored me. Sheba fixed her gaze on a distant point. "Nyva stayed with me for the weekend, but then she went back to him. I tried to tell her he would do it again, that he'd never change, but she wouldn't listen. She was sure it was just because he'd had too much to drink.

"Two weeks later, she was back here again. This time, he had dislocated her shoulder. I took her to the hospital and got her fixed up. She came back here and stayed with me for a week. I thought she finally understood, but I was wrong. She went back to him *again*."

"Why would she do that?" Hank said.

"How can I explain? I know what she was going through because I was there once, too. It's different when you're in the middle of it. You tell yourself it was just one time. He says he's sorry, and you believe it. You believe he wants to change. There's shame involved, too. You don't want people to know the bad decisions you've made. You want everything to be perfect, so you keep pretending it is, even though the world's falling apart around you."

"So that's when you decided you had to kill him?" said Hank.

Sheba laughed quietly, and wiped her tears again. "Not then, not exactly. We discussed it. I joked with her that we should kill him, and that between the two of us, we'd have all of his money. I'd already taken half of it, you know."

"We get it," I said. "But that was months ago. It didn't take you that long to come up with this master plan." I held up the bottle. "If it did, you've got more problems than I thought."

"No," she said. "It wasn't like that. We just talked about the idea, we didn't actually plan anything out. Like I said, she was only here for a week. Then she went back to him again."

"So what happened?" said Hank. "I don't understand. You're going around in circles."

"That's exactly what happened," she said. "Going in circles. That's what it's like for a woman in an abusive relationship. It's a cycle that just keeps going, until she finally breaks it off or he kills her. I tried to help her. I told Nyva we'd call the cops, that we would sue him, even that we'd hire a killer. Every time she came to me, I told her these things, but then after a few days, she'd be gone. Right back into his arms."

"Skip ahead," said Hank. "To the relevant part."

Sheba nodded. She tossed her tissue on the table and grabbed a fresh one. She blew her cute little dryad nose and then started up again:

"I had given up on her. I had tried to help Nyva any way I could, but she just kept going back to Pretty Boy. She didn't have the strength to cut the ties. I even considered hiring a hitman without her approval, but I knew she'd never forgive me if I had him killed. Then the other day, Nyva called me. She wanted to meet for coffee and talk about things. I met her at the café downstairs. I knew as soon as I saw her that something had changed."

"Did he beat her again?" said Hank.

"No, not at all. In fact, she looked healthier than I had seen her in a long time. The fact was that Pretty Boy had *stopped* beating her. That was because Pretty Boy had lost interest in her. Nyva had finally learned about Pretty Boy's other *tastes*. She'd learned about his affairs."

A FOOL THERE WAS

"Wait a minute," said Hank. "You're telling me that after months of that piece of garbage beating her, the thing that changed her mind about him was *an affair?*"

"That's exactly what I'm telling you. See, Nyva considered herself strong enough to take Pretty Boy's abuse. She thought she could take it, and that she could change him. It took the affairs to make her realize that he truly didn't care about her at all."

"So you came up with this together?" Hank said. "You both decided to poison him?"

"No. After meeting at the café, we came up here to talk. On the way up, Nyva showed me be the bottle of poison and told me what she had done. She had *already killed him*."

We let that statement hang in the air for a minute. Then I said:

"You played me like a harp, didn't you? The day I came here, you pretended like you thought I was the killer. What a fool I am!"

"I'm sorry, Sam. I didn't plan it that way. I couldn't have planned it any better if I had, though. You see, I was sure my sister would go to prison. Then, when the police announced that they believed you were the killer, I saw a chance for her. That's when I came up with the plan for Nyva to leave the country. I didn't mean for you to take the fall, I just wanted to buy her some time. I wanted to muddy the waters, so they'd never pick up the trail. But then she came back. She said she couldn't live on the run. She'd rather face the Elders and hope they gave her leniency, if it came to that."

"But she never confessed!" I shouted. "She was going to let me hang. Are you two completely rotten?"

"No! We were just waiting to see what happened. We figured the cops would let you go for lack of evidence. Then Nyva wouldn't have to speak up and risk going to prison. We were just playing it safe, that's all."

"Where is your sister now?" said Hank.

"In the back room."

I tossed Hank the bottle as I ran past them, into the hall. When I reached the door to the bedroom, it was locked. I smashed into it with my shoulder, but it was a security door with a steel core and double deadbolts. I dug into my pocket looking for my lock picks, but then remembered Hank still had my kit. By then, he was already behind me.

"Move outta the way," Hank grumbled. I stepped aside and he kicked the door violently. It shuddered under his attack. I heard the steel deadbolts creaking like the Titanic right before it sank. He kicked it again, and the steel core folded inward like an aluminum can. The wood paneling crackled, the deadbolts ripped out of the jamb, and the door exploded inward. It slammed against the inside wall. It rested there, partially embedded in the sheetrock, hanging slightly askew on the twisted hinges. We barged into the room.

Nyva was nowhere in sight. Hank rushed to check the bathroom. By the time he came out, I was already looking down the fire escape attached to the balcony. Nothing. She was gone.

Sheba appeared in the doorway behind us, and I glared at her. "Nice trick, tell us that story to buy your sister some time," I said. "Was any of it true?"

Hank frowned. He hadn't even considered the fact that Sheba might have been lying to us.

A FOOL THERE WAS

"Of course it was," she protested. "Nyva may be the killer, but that doesn't mean I'm going to let her go to prison. Pretty Boy deserved to die!"

Hank stepped away from the balcony and ripped out his cell phone. He tapped the screen and said, "Call Gen!" To my surprise, it actually worked.

Hank quickly told Gen to put out an alert on Nyva, and promised to explain everything shortly. When that was done, he fixed Sheba with an angry glare. He pulled out a pair of handcuffs, and held them out.

"Put these on."

"You wouldn't dare," she said. "You can't arrest me. I didn't do anything."

"Resisting arrest," Hank said. "Interfering with a murder investigation. The longer you keep me waiting, the more charges I'll think up."

Sheba snatched the cuffs out of his hand and locked them on her wrists. "Fine, arrest me," she said defiantly. "My lawyers get paid more in an hour than you do in a month. I'll be back home by sunrise."

"We'll see," Hank said with a grimace. "Let's get moving."

After Hank had Sheba locked up, we parted ways for the night. I rented a car and took the long way home, driving across the Golden Gate and up a secret road through Muir Woods. It was late, nearly six p.m. by the time I got home.

I hadn't slept all day, and even though it was getting dark, I wanted to crash. But I was also half-starved, so I decided to cook something up. I was in the mood for pizza, but not the junk food they deliver. I have a big brick pizza oven next to the hot tub. There's no beating a hand-tossed crust. It takes a while to let the dough rise, but being extra hungry just makes the meal that much more satisfying. I prepped the toppings and sipped some wine while I waited for the dough to rise.

I made the pizza Mediterranean style, with roasted peppers, sun dried tomatoes, and marinated artichoke hearts on a bed of spinach and feta cheese. I kept the red sauce simple with garlic, oregano, and a pinch of sea salt. When I smelled the flavor coming out of that brick oven, I started slavering. When I bit into the first slice, it was pure heaven. It took me right back to those early days, living on the roof of that little Italian diner. Chef Antonio would've been proud.

I put the rest of the pie on a platter next to the hot tub and settled into the hot, churning waters with a glass of Petite Sirah and a half-empty bottle within easy reach. With my glass of wine in one hand and a slice of pie in the other, I leaned back and let the bubbling waters ease my worries away.

An hour later, there were only two slices of pizza left and the bottle was empty. I had been mulling things over in my head, considering the holes left in our case. We had our killer now, or supposedly did. It was just a matter of waiting for the cops to catch up with her. Once they had Nyva in custody, the whole truth would come out. Then we'd know if she was really the killer, and just how much Sheba had to do with the whole thing. In the meanwhile, I had a few more questions. Like who had killed Gordy? And where was the diamond?

The obvious answer to the first question seemed to be Skully Marcozi. He'd wanted the technology that Pretty Boy and Gordy had been working on. That was all the motive a goblin like Skully needed for murder. I was sure he had killed for a whole lot less in the past. Not that I had any idea what that technology actually was. I didn't even have the prints anymore. Gen had somehow ended up with those. I could only assume the police were working on figuring that out.

I went to bed feeling pretty good about everything in general. There were only two things bothering me. The first was that the cops still had my car. I knew that I'd get it back eventually, but it was a minor irritation nonetheless. A goblin's car is part of his identity. When it's missing, things just don't seem right. The second thing bothering me was that even though the case was almost closed, I still didn't know how I was going to *get paid*. I'd wasted a lot of time on this case. I had also risked my life and put up with a considerable amount of abuse at the hands of a certain big green moron named Hank. Somewhere, somehow, there had to be a paycheck in there for me. It was just a matter of figuring out where.

Sleeping on it didn't help. In fact, I overslept. When I woke, I realized I had twenty minutes to get topside before Skully's hearing, otherwise I wouldn't even be able to testify. The last thing I wanted was for Skully to walk on some sort of technicality. I knew that as soon as he was back on the streets, I'd be as good as dead. I might be able to duck him for a while, but with Skully's resources, it was only a matter of time until he caught up to me. If there's one thing a goblin hates more than being poor, it's being dead.

I called Hank on my way into town and he offered to give me a lift from the access point south of the Golden Gate Bridge, just at the edge of the Canal District. I had to abandon my rental car there. I was pretty sure I'd never see it again, but I wasn't too worried about it. That's why I always buy insurance.

I took the elevator up into a little coffee shop in the Sea Cliff District, and found Hank, Mickey, and Gen waiting for me. It was pouring rain outside, blowing like a hurricane. We all crawled into Hank's rusty old Blazer, and he drove us across town, to the Ebon Tower on Telegraph Hill where the hearing was scheduled.

Hank's windows didn't seal all the way, and since I had to sit in the back seat, the icy wind and splashes of rain kept blasting me in the face all the way across town. I bit my tongue. I'd already given Hank enough trouble about his financial situation, so there was no point in rubbing it in. If he cared about money, all he had to do was quit being Steward and get a real job. Fat chance of that ever happening.

Hank took his phone out and dropped it into a cup holder. "Turn your phones off or leave them in the car," he said. "The elders don't like court interruptions."

I silenced mine. Mickey and Gen left theirs next to Hank's.

When we finally arrived, the rain had stopped, but it was still cold and blustery. In fact, the wind was blowing even harder up on Telegraph Hill than it had been on the coast. I climbed out of the Blazer and stood there in the parking lot, my trench coat wrapped tight against the wind, staring up at the Ebon Tower. I had never seen it before in person.

It was impressive, ominous and looming, like the weather. I found a mood of melancholy sadness washing over me as I noted the dark clouds churning in the sky behind it. I could feel the magic of the place, but it wasn't just normal magic. It wasn't vibrant and lively. It was *power,* with all its capacity for good or evil, for judgment and destruction; the same kind humans have in their fortresses of concrete and iron defended

A FOOL THERE WAS

by jet fighters and nuclear weapons. It made me feel strangely insignificant.

The Ebon Tower is made of literal ebony, magically grown into the shape of a wizard's tower two hundred feet tall. It looks as black and shiny as obsidian from a distance -unless of course you're human, and then you can't see it at all- but up close, you can see every grain and striation in the wood. You can see knots smoothed over by time and centuries of wind and rain, and streaks of color that almost look like stripes of frosted glass melded with the dark hardwood. All of this is oddly accentuated by the white structure that stands at the very front of the Ebon Tower, a human landmark known as the Coit Tower. In fact, the only way *into* the Ebon Tower is through a secret passage in the Coit Tower.

I hadn't noticed my companions had gone ahead without me until I felt Gen's warm touch on my hand. "Come on, Sam," she said, taking me by the hand. "It's freezing out here. Let's get inside."

She squeezed my hand and it helped a little. Normally, I would have taken it the wrong way. Even as a gesture of friendship, I would have taken it as a proposition. I would have done it on purpose. I'd have done it to make her uncomfortable, to gain control over her, and to lay the course for something that might happen someday in the future. But not this time. For some strange reason, I felt *wrong* about everything that was about to happen. With every step I took towards that tower, I felt a fear I'd never known before building inside of me, urging me to turn and run the other way.

It's a spell, I told myself. *The Elders do this so they can keep the rest of us in our places. Nobody will challenge them that way, because they're too afraid... It's just a spell...*

Maybe. Then again, maybe not. I can usually sense magic, at least to some degree. A spell is like a trickle of energy, like the sound of a running faucet in the next room. It's the kind of thing you can completely overlook unless you're paying attention. This wasn't like that. If magic is a dripping faucet, I was standing on the edge of a raging river. Yes, there was magic there, it just wasn't the kind I was used to, and I didn't like it one bit.

We hurried up the slope and caught up with Hank and Mickey just outside the Coit Tower. We were already late, so there was no time to examine the murals or read about the history of the place. We simply rushed into the main entrance and then hurried through a pair of magical arches in the far wall. The air shimmered around us. Just like that, we were standing inside the Ebon Tower.

We stood in a long lobby, not much different from any other government building. The place had marble floors, dark ebony walls decorated with tapestries and paintings, and delicately embroidered carpets that ran the length of the hall, which stretched out in either direction in a long, sweeping curve. Torches burned in sconces every few yards, and doorways opened up here and there, but the entrance to the courtroom was directly in front of us: two large ebony doors with brass handles, guarded by two dangerous-looking wizards with long beards wearing black robes. Once again, I felt the urge to tuck tail and run. Once again, for some strange reason, I resisted that urge.

A FOOL THERE WAS

I had expected a large hearing, but to my surprise there were only a dozen people seated inside the courtroom. Here and there, reporters stood along the aisles and against the outside walls readying their cameras and recorders. On the tall, imposing stage at the front of the room, twelve elders had settled into their ebony thrones. Before them, Skully sat at a table with his lawyers. Adjacent to him, at another table, sat Zane Bossa -the chief of police- with another group of attorneys.

We hurried to the front of the room. Just as we took our seats, a loud female voice announced, "Welcome to the one hundred and thirty-first session of the Elder's Council. Bailiffs, secure the courtroom!"

There was a booming sound as the doors slammed shut behind us. The noise echoed back and forth in the gloomy courtroom. Then the voice continued: "Ladies and gentlemen, rise for the judges!"

We all took our feet and listened patiently as the voice listed off the names of the judges. Then it named Skully as the defendant, and Bossa as the prosecutor. Hank wasn't mentioned at all, but he didn't seem to mind.

At last, we took our seats and the voice declared the beginning of the trial. Skully's attorney climbed the stairs to a podium on the right side of the stage, and the chief took the podium on the left.

"Honorable Elders," said the lawyer, "I come to you today in defense of my client, Skully Marcozi. He, a poor innocent businessman who has done no harm to anyone, as his record will clearly attest, stands accused of the most heinous crimes of not only theft, but also murder! I will prove to you beyond the shadow of a doubt that my client is innocent of all charges. Not only that, but that he is the victim of a vicious smear campaign on the part of the undercity police department."

"Prosecutor!" called one of the judges. "Make your case!"

The chief cleared his throat. "I'd like to submit exhibit 'A' into evidence," said Zane Bossa. "This envelope contains a copy of Skully Marcozi's record, which demonstrates an extensive and flagrant disregard of the law-"

"Objection!" shouted the lawyer. "My client has never been convicted of any major crime!"

"Convicted or not, he's been implicated in cases of everything from racketeering and extortion to murder," said the chief. "Skully Marcozi's lack of convictions is not evidence of absence, but rather indicative of a serious pattern of criminal behavior."

"We'll review the exhibit later," said one of the Elders. "Prosecutor, I hope you have more up your sleeve than vague accusations."

"Of course," said the chief. "May I present 'Exhibit B.' This is the record of Skully's arrest on suspicion of murder, and his subsequent escape. If nothing else, the court should find satisfactory evidence to convict Mr. Marcozi as the fugitive he is."

Skully's lawyer wisely remained silent for this part. It's never good to dispute a crime the cops have already proven. Better to find a way to trivialize it later, or to trivialize the cops themselves.

I could see how high-paid lawyers like Skully's earned their keep. Not that I'd have paid them. I'm not an idiot like Skully or Pretty Boy. If I needed a lawyer, I'd do it myself. The chief

A FOOL THERE WAS

went on to submit various exhibits and then called on witnesses. An eyewitness testified seeing Skully near the lab where Gordy was murdered. Another saw him fighting with the police at the depot.

Eventually, they called me to testify about what I knew. Despite the fact that my nerves had been eating me up for the last hour, when I took the podium, I felt strangely relaxed. I told them about Gordy's murder, about the way someone had tortured him and how he'd told me about the lockbox. I told them about my first interaction with Skully, when he'd threatened to kill me at the depot. Then I told them about the blueprints I had found, and the strange spider device inside the lab.

"Do you have these blueprints?" said of the Elders. It was Thom, the eldest of the Bolger twins, the only gnomes ever to become Elders.

"Here!" the chief called out, shuffling through his pile of folders. He held it out, and a bailiff took it from him and handed it to Thom. The Elder scanned it and then passed it on. The rest of the Elders passed it back and forth amongst themselves, murmuring.

"What does it do?" said his brother, Skip Bolger. The chief hesitated.

"Well?" said another Elder, a high-elf woman with short, golden hair. "Don't leave us in suspense."

"Honestly, nothing," the chief said with a resigned tone.

"What?"

"I'm sorry, your honors. As far as we can tell, the device won't work. Our technicians think it was designed to look like some sort of weapon, but... well, it's just *not*."

"Do you mean the device is nonfunctional? That it's incomplete?"

He lowered his eye. "It's just a bunch of metal and computer parts welded together. It's really nothing more than useless junk. Or modern art, perhaps. At the very most, my technicians say this machine can throw off some sparks."

I glanced at Skully, and saw his eyes widen. His hands flexed into fists and then he slowly forced them open. Although this information was clearly very upsetting to him, he stared straight ahead and forced himself to relax before anyone else noticed his displeasure.

"Don't forget the diamond!" I blurted out. The Elders looked at me, and then back at the chief. He hesitated, until they urged him to get on with it. He shot me a venomous look.

"There have been rumors," Bossa said. "Unsubstantiated rumors, I hasten to add, that Pretty Boy was in possession of a certain diamond worth several million dollars. A diamond which has allegedly been stolen."

"And what does this have to do with this case?"

"If you look at the prints, it does appear that this machine has a socket designed to fit the diamond in question. It has been speculated that perhaps Skully and Gordy had a dispute over the diamond-"

"Speculated!" shouted the lawyer. "Chief, do you have anything besides speculation? Or do you expect this most honorable court to lock up an innocent man based on these fairy tales?"

"I can't prove it yet," the chief said uncomfortably, at which point the lawyer began to laugh loudly.

A FOOL THERE WAS

"He can't prove anything. Your honors, I beg you to dismiss this ludicrous case before it taints your courtroom."

"The defense has a valid point," said one of the Elders. "Chief, do you have *anything* in the way of actual evidence?"

"I was going to get to that," said the Chief. "Exhibit G." He produced an envelope and handed it to the bailiff. One of the Elders opened it, and pulled out a small, shiny object. He held it aloft, and we all gasped. It was the diamond.

"Where did you find this?"

"Acting on the warrant provided by this court, we searched the residence and business offices of the defendant. We found that in one of his safes." I heard gasps, and a clamor of murmuring voices. The Elders passed the stone around, each examining it in turn. One of them held it out in his palm and muttered some sort of a spell. The diamond began to glow with a yellowish hue.

"It's fake," he announced.

There was an immediate uproar. The Elders all examined the stone again, and then at last called the court back to order. The Grand Master sighed loudly.

"Chief, do you have any *real* evidence to present at this hearing today?'

Chief Bossa grimaced. "Exhibit B," he mumbled.

"Ah, yes, the part about Skully's escape from your jail. I'm beginning to understand his reasons quite clearly. Most innocent men yearn for their freedom, wouldn't you say?"

The chief glared at me. "Yes, your honor."

The Elder sighed. "The court will adjourn for a brief discourse."

With that, the judges filed out of the room.

I glanced over at Skully and saw him staring back at me, grinning from ear to ear. He made a sliding motion across his throat with his index finger, and then pointed at me. I suddenly knew exactly why I'd had that bad feeling all afternoon. By testifying against him, I had just signed my own death warrant. If he went free, I probably wouldn't live another week.

Chapter 16

It took five minutes for the Elders to reach a decision. The ethereal voice in the rafters called the courtroom to order as the judges filed in and took their seats. The Grand Master, chief among the Elders, handed down the sentence. He was a very old man, so old and so *changed* by magic that he didn't really look human at all. His face was short and narrow, like a gnome's, but his eyes were the size of a hoot-owl's. In fact, with his long hair and beard covering most of his face, he really looked more like a pair of eyeballs staring out of a puffy white cloud than anything else.

"Skully Marcozi," he began. "On the accusation of murder, theft, and other miscellaneous charges, the court finds you *not guilty*. For the crime of escaping jail, the court finds you guilty and sentences you to time served. For the crime of assault and battery, the court finds you *guilty,* and hereby sentences you to one year prison time, eligible for parole in six months."

I heard gasps all around me. I felt a weight lift off my shoulders. I had six months to live. Six months to come up with some sort of escape plan. It wasn't ideal, but it was better than the alternative. Skully's smile vanished. He smacked his fist down on the table and gave his lawyer a furious glare. The man immediately began to deflect, and for good reason. Skully had never been convicted of anything. This was a permanent stain on his record. I expected that lawyer would probably be dead by morning.

Hank's massive hand clapped down on my shoulder and I nearly jumped out of my skin. "That's it," he said. "Let's go."

We filed out of the courtroom and into the lobby, where the reporters were all screaming for interviews. They asked Hank about the verdict and he said it was a good start. Gen said, "No comment."

"What about you?" one of them said, pointing his camera in my direction. "If not for your testimony, Skully would have gone free again."

"I only did what I had to," I said meekly. "I was hired to do a job, and I won't quit until that job's done." I know opportunity when I smell it. I stared directly into the camera. "That's Snyvvle, with a Y. Sam Snyvvle, Private Investigator."

"You're very brave, Mr. Snyvvle," said a fiery-haired nymph with long ears and bright green eyes like two glowing emeralds. She held out a microphone. "Are you worried about what will happen when Skully Marcozi gets out of prison?"

"I'll worry about that when it happens," I said. "For now, I'm worried about your dehydration problem."

"Excuse me?"

"There's a bar just down the street. Let's get a drink or ten."

She signaled to her cameraman that the interview was over. "Perhaps another time," she said to me. "I'm on the air in twenty minutes."

"Sure thing, dollface. Here's my card."

"Oh, no need for that," she said with a wink. "You're Sam Snyvvle, Private Investigator." She smiled as she turned away, and I took that as a promising sign.

A FOOL THERE WAS

We left the tower and wandered back down to the parking lot in silence. We were all frustrated and disappointed. We knew that Skully was guilty of far more than just attacking me, but we had no way to prove it. If only we'd had more time...

"Just a minute!" a voice shouted behind us. "Stop right there!" It was the chief.

We turned and waited for Bossa at the edge of the parking lot, the wind whipping up our coats, icy chills crawling up and down the backs of our necks. I had to hold onto my hat for fear of it blowing away. The chief stomped down the path and then glared at us one by one as he caught up.

"Do you people have any idea what you've done?"

"It's not their fault," Gen said quickly. "They did everything they could-"

The chief silenced her with a glare. "You've destroyed my case," he snarled. "I could've put Skully Marcozi away for good. I was this close to having him on a murder rap, and he beat it because of you morons."

"You brought in the Elders," Hank said flatly. "You handed him over to them before you even had a case. If anybody screwed this up, it was you."

"Oh, you're a real wiseguy, Mossberg. You know what I ought to do? I ought to arrest you. That way I can at least make sure you're doing time in Skully's cell block."

"Why don't you try?" Hank snarled, flexing his hands into fists.

They were seconds from coming to blows, but at that very second, we all heard a phone ringing in the distance. It seemed to be coming from Hank's Blazer. Mickey glanced at Hank.

"Is that your cell?" he said.

"Sounds like it," Hank grunted. "I left it in the car."

"It might be Tas. I'll get it!"

As Mickey raced across the parking lot, Hank turned his attention back to the chief. "It seems to me that the best thing you can do is stay out of our way before you screw this up any worse."

"Fat chance," the chief growled.

"Fat is right. We already solved Pretty Boy's murder while you were back at the precinct inhaling donuts. We will have Nyva Marcozi in custody soon and by then, we'll probably have hard evidence against Skully, too. The best thing you can do for anyone is to go back to your desk and eat a few more extra large pizzas."

The chief raised his fist threateningly.

The Blazer exploded behind us.

It came out of nowhere. The bomb must have been attached to the light switch, because I'm pretty sure I remember hearing Mickey open the door just as it happened. How could I forget the squeaking sound of Hank's hinges? The next thing anyone knew, a fifty foot fireball went roaring up into the sky, followed by a billowing tower of acrid black smoke.

The shockwave hit me so hard that I fell on my ass. My ears were ringing. Gen was on the ground next to me, and the chief was behind us. I pushed up to a sitting position and saw Hank standing there, a massive black silhouette against the fiery brightness of the explosion. His trench coat fluttered back in the breeze. His hat was gone. He wasn't moving. He just stood there, staring, disbelieving.

A FOOL THERE WAS

Bits and pieces of rusty metal began raining down around us, and a spare tire went rolling down the hill. I helped Gen to her feet.

"Hank?" she said stepping past me, her limp a bit more pronounced after her fall. "Are you okay?"

She walked up to him and touched him lightly on the arm, but he didn't move. He just stared into the licking flames, his chest slowly rising and falling with his breath. The Blazer had been incinerated. There was nothing left but a melted engine block with two broken axles. There was no chance for Mickey. No chance at all. He must have been vaporized before we even heard the sound of the explosion.

The chief came up behind us, his jaw hanging open, his big bloodshot eye rapidly blinking.

"I'm... I, uh... I'll call for backup." He wandered away, digging through his pockets, looking for his cell phone.

"You couldn't have done anything," Gen said. "It's not your fault, Hank."

"She's right," I said. "This was Skully's doing. That bomb was meant for you, Hank."

He turned his head slowly and looked at me out of the corner of his eye. I felt a shiver run down my spine. Something had changed in the Steward's face. He didn't look human anymore. Hell, he didn't even look fae. He looked like a wild animal, a wolf or a lion maybe; some terrifyingly powerful and intelligent beast with one sole purpose in life: *to kill*.

He turned and went marching past us, back towards the tower. I glanced at Gen, and she at me. It took us a second to register what he was doing. By then, Hank had begun to run.

"We have to stop him," Gen said. "He's going to kill Skully."

I frowned. "And we should stop him why?"

She glared at me. "Because he'll go to prison, you idiot." She broke into a run. I sighed and took off after her.

I'm pretty light on my feet, but I was shocked to see how fast Gen could move. She had a slight hitch in her step because of that old injury to her hip, but even that didn't seem to slow her down. I had a hard time just keeping up. By then, Hank had a hundred yards on us. He was already inside the tower, and we were only halfway there. Gen put on a burst of speed and vanished into the shadowy interior. I arrived a few seconds later, panting and blinking against the darkness. I located the secret entrance and stepped through the arches.

The Ebon Tower was empty now, and quiet, but otherwise it was exactly as it had been before. The torches still burned in their sconces. The doors to the courtroom stood open. I hurried inside, following Gen, and saw Hank at the far end of the room, staring up at the empty thrones. Gen was just ahead of me, standing in the aisle. She turned to look at me and shook her head. She was crying.

"They're gone?" I said quietly. Gen nodded. She wiped the tears from her cheeks. I went to her side and put an arm around her. We both turned to stare at Hank. A minute passed in complete silence, and then another. Finally, I felt like I had to say something.

"Let's go, Hank," I said. "There's nothing we can do here. We'll get Skully later."

Hank's shoulders lifted as he took a deep breath. He turned toward us, and for a second it looked like he would join us. Then he turned aside and before we knew it, had taken the stairs four at a time up to the dais. Hank stepped up to one

A FOOL THERE WAS

of the thrones and threw his head back, roaring violently. The walls shook around us, and I had to fight my instinctive urge to release my bladder.

Hank bent forward and lifted one of the thrones in the air. With a roar, he smashed it down on top of the next one. Gen whimpered in fright as the four hundred pound thrones disintegrated into slivers. Hank wasn't through yet. He lifted another and threw it against the back wall. It shattered into kindling and left a three-foot hole where several large stones had busted out.

The Steward turned and kicked another throne. It rose slightly on two legs and then slid sideways across the stage. That only seemed to piss him off even more. Hank picked it up and hurled it out into the seats off to our left. The courtroom filled with the sound of snapping wood as the smaller chairs crumbled beneath its weight.

Hank hammered two more of the chairs together, crushing them into bits, and then stood staring at the others. To my surprise, he simply turned his back and came walking down the stairs towards us. Gen and I stared at him as he brushed past us and headed for the exit. As one, we took off after him.

The weight lifted as we stepped back outside. The wind had died down and the air seemed to have cleared. I actually saw a few stars peeking down through the breaks in the clouds. The undercity police were already fast at work, cleaning up the debris from the explosion. Hank and Gen walked down the path to give them a statement, and I used the opportunity to call a taxi. After that, I called Information to get the number for Hank's friend Tas, a gnome computer hacker who lives in

Marin. I'd never met him, but I had heard of him. Everyone has heard of Tas.

Tas answered right away, and I explained what had happened. He was understandably shaken. "How about Hank?" he said. "He's all right?"

"He'll be fine," I said. "Once he breaks Skully's neck, anyway."

"Tell him I got the information he wanted. I found the receipt for aspartame he was looking for. Only it wasn't Sheba Marcozi, it was Nyva."

"We already know," I said. "Send Hank a copy. He can use it to help prosecute her." I'd already learned my lesson from Skully's hearing. *Document everything.* That was going to be my new motto. Maybe I could combine them: *Think ahead and document everything.*

No. That sounded like crap. I got off the phone at the same time the taxi pulled up. Hank and Gen had finished giving their statements, so I waved them over.

"Good thinking," Hank said. "Can you give me a lift?"

"I'll give you more than that," I said. "You two are coming home with me."

They glanced at each other. "I don't know," Gen said. "I have laundry to do, and cleaning-"

"Your laundry isn't going anywhere," I said. "Besides, for all we know Skully's goons are waiting for you at home right now. I can't have that on my conscience. You two are staying at my place. I insist."

"There's another thing," Hank said reluctantly. "I have to notify Mickey's parents."

"Oh, Hank," Gen said. "Let the police handle it."

A FOOL THERE WAS

Hank shook his head adamantly. "Nope, Mickey was my deputy. I owe him that much."

"All right then," I said. "We'll go with you."

That settled it. We all climbed into the cab and headed downtown, to the access point nearest the undercity tram depot.

It took an hour to locate Mickey's parents and break the news to them. They were understandably heartbroken, and none too happy with Hank for letting Mickey have the job in the first place. I knew they'd get over it. For the most part, fae creatures reincarnate. Or at least they think they do. And since many of them live for hundreds or even thousands of years, death eventually becomes a relatively trivial matter.

I guess deep down it doesn't matter what you believe in, as long as you believe in *something*. It's not death that's terrifying, it's an eternity of *nothingness*. Nobody wants to go from sentience to nothingness without any explanations. As long as it's not that, fae can handle death.

Of course, none of that does much good in the midst of the grief. The best Hank could do was to apologize, and promise to find the man who'd taken Mickey's life and bring him to justice. They were grateful for that much, at least.

During the conversation, I had called an undercity car rental agency and ordered a sedan delivered to the residence. It was waiting for us outside when we left.

"Nice car," Hank said as we crawled inside. "I didn't realize these places deliver."

"They'll do anything for a price," I said. I glanced at Gen. "Speaking of which, this wouldn't be necessary if *someone* hadn't impounded my car."

"Your car was impounded?" Gen said. "I'll look into it. No promises."

"Fair enough."

I thought about mentioning my lockpicking kit to Hank, and dismissed the idea. He had enough on his mind. I had more picks at home.

I drove back through the Canal District, a little quicker this time since the creeps down there wouldn't recognize my rental car. I gave Gen a heart attack on a couple of hairpin corners, but other than that we made it through without a scratch. We pulled in to my driveway at three a.m.

"Very impressive," Gen said as we stepped through the front door. "I had no idea you had a place up here."

"Hank knew," I said with a grin. He smiled, ever so slightly.

"Come on," I said. "The bar's over here."

Hank leaned up against the counter and Gen settled onto a stool. I stepped around behind the bar and pulled out a good bottle of scotch and some shot glasses. "Wine for me, if you don't mind," Gen said.

"Sure thing, dollface." I brought out a rare vintage of chardonnay and her eyes lit up. She went to work on a glass, and I poured several shot glasses for Hank and me. We started drinking. We were halfway through the second bottle before he finally loosened up. It was like pouring alcohol down a black hole. I thought it might never take effect.

"I never should've let Mickey have that job," he said suddenly. We had been talking about other things up until that point; the weather, the 49ers, whatever else we could think of that didn't have to do with Mickey or the case. Gen and I stared at him, listening intently. The lights were low and I had some

A FOOL THERE WAS

soft jazz music playing quietly in the background. Hank's voice was a low rumble.

"I told him it was dangerous. I told him people get killed doing this work, but he wouldn't back down."

"Mickey was a grown man," Gen said. "He was free to make his own choices, Hank. He knew the job was dangerous. It wasn't up to you to make that decision for him."

I felt guilt welling up inside me as she spoke. I suddenly felt terrible about giving him such a hard time. The whole time I'd known him, I had treated Mickey like a little kid. I had called him names and made fun of him. Now the poor guy was dead.

"I could've said *no*," Hank said.

"No, you couldn't," Gen argued. "You *needed* his help. And he did a fine job, too!"

Hank smiled slightly. "That he did," he said. He downed another shot. "My office has never been so organized."

I raised my shot glass. "To Mickey," I said. "The only dwarf I ever met with no beard, but he was one helluva cop."

"To Mickey," they echoed. Hank threw back another shot and slammed the glass down on the bar. He shifted slightly, and I could tell he was a little off balance. He'd had too much to drink. We all had.

"You know what gets me?" he said. "Do you know why Mickey wanted that job? Do you?"

We stared at him.

"To find a girlfriend," Hank snarled. "That's all he wanted. Not to be a hero, or to prove anything. He just wanted to meet a nice girl."

Gen couldn't take it anymore. She started bawling. I was right behind her. I bent down below the counter, pretending to be looking for a towel as I wiped the moisture from my eyes on the back of my sleeve.

When I got back up, Gen had her head in her hands and her shoulders were shaking with sobs. Hank was staring at the second empty bottle like he wanted to kill it, but it wasn't the bottle he saw there. It was Skully Marcozi. I silently promised myself that no matter how else this came out, I'd make sure he succeeded at that.

I don't remember exactly when we wandered off to bed. When I woke up that afternoon with a skull-splitting headache and a mouth as dry as the Sahara, I wandered down the hall and found Hank sleeping on the sofa. That was when I remembered that Gen had taken the spare room. I had assured her the night before that there was room for both of us in my bed, and she'd joked that if it was so big, maybe Hank should sleep there with me. Hank hadn't seen the humor.

I started a pot of coffee and dug some food out of the fridge. Twenty minutes later, I had steaming mugs of coffee waiting for them, along with omelets with diced onion, bell pepper, cheddar, parmesan, and just a touch of garlic. It's one of my own recipes, and surprisingly tasty. Hank was a little disappointed at the lack of meat, but he didn't grumble too much. Mostly, he just wanted some aspirin, which I was only too happy to share.

As we finished our meal, Gen spoke up:

"Aside from the lack of evidence, it looks like this case is mostly wrapped up," she said. "My report will show that Nyva Marcozi poisoned her husband, and then covered up the crime with the help of her sister."

"What about Gordy?" said Hank.

A FOOL THERE WAS

"Well, we know Skully killed him. We just can't prove it yet. But both murders are solved, as far as I'm concerned."

"We're still thin on motive," said Hank.

"That's not the only thing that's thin," I added. They both looked at me inquisitively. I explained: "Our theory is that Skully killed Gordy for the diamond. Correct?"

"Correct," said Gen.

"Then what happened to the real diamond? The one Skully had was a fake."

Gen's eyes widened. "I forgot about that."

"I don't think Skully knew it, either," I added. "From the way he looked at the trial, he wasn't too happy when the fake was discovered."

"He wasn't," Hank said. "Looked like he wanted to fly off the handle, right there in court."

"So how's it all connected?" I said.

"It's the diamond," said Gen. "It has to be."

"But that wasn't why Nyva killed Pretty Boy. And according to Freddie the Fist, the diamond was still in the safe after she did it. So what happened to it?"

"Nyva -or Sheba- took it and replaced it with a fake," said Gen. "Maybe they both did it together."

"That's a decent theory," said Hank. "Nyva could easily have known about the diamond. Between her and her sister, they might have decided to kill Pretty Boy, steal the diamond, and replace it with a fake."

"So how did Skully end up with the fake?" said Gen.

I leaned back against the counter and crossed my arms. "Picture this: Maybe Gordy set the whole thing up as a scheme to steal the diamond. He knew that it was just a matter of time until Pretty Boy found out his machine was a fake, but he planned to be long gone by then. Once Gordy knew that Pretty Boy was keeping the diamond in his safe, all he had to do was break into the flat and steal it. Unfortunately for Gordy, someone else had already killed Pretty Boy and made the swap."

"But then why shoot Pretty Boy?" said Gen. "He was already dead from poison."

"And you're overlooking something else," Hank added. "What does Skully have to do with any of this? How is he connected to Gordy?"

"Gordy was working for Skully's brother," said Gen. "Maybe Skully knew about."

"No, Gordy was *conning* Pretty Boy," I corrected. "Skully must have got wind of it and wanted in on the action."

"And when Gordy tried to steal the diamond and make a run for it, Skully was waiting," said Hank.

"Exactly. Gordy went back to the lab after stealing the fake diamond, and that's where Skully caught up with him. Skully killed Gordy and stole the fake diamond thinking it was the real one."

"And the blueprints?" said Gen.

"Skully wanted those too, obviously," I said. "Maybe he believed the machine would actually work."

We all fell silent for a while, considering it from every angle. "It all fits," Gen said at last.

"Except that we can't prove it," said Hank. "We can't prove it was Gordy who shot Pretty Boy, and we can't prove Skully killed Gordy. Legally speaking, we've got nothing."

"Then we get proof," I said.

"How?" said Gen.

A FOOL THERE WAS

"We need the diamond," said Hank. "The Scarlet Tear will prove the motive behind all this. Sheba or Nyva must have it hidden somewhere."

"And the gun," I said. "That gun will tie Gordy to Pretty Boy. And of course, the knife Skully used to torture Gordy. That should buy Skully a few more years behind bars, too."

Hank looked at Gen. "We'll need to search every piece of property Pretty Boy and his wives own if we want that diamond. Same with Skully, for the knife. Can you get warrants?"

"I'll talk to one of the Elders... one whose chair you *didn't break*. The Bolger brothers, maybe."

"You two work on that," I said. "I'll check the lab again; see if we missed a clue there. Maybe Gordy's gun is still there somewhere."

Chapter 17

I had my doubts about Hank and Gen finding the knife that had killed Gordy, because Skully was smart enough to have the weapon destroyed right away. On the other hand, it was *possible* that Gordy had stashed the gun he'd used on Pretty Boy. That wouldn't exactly seal the case either, but it would be a big step towards tying the whole case into one cohesive story. I figured that if Gordy had gone straight back to the lab after shooting Pretty Boy, then maybe the gun was there somewhere. If I could find that gun and prove Gordy's connection, that would be a huge step forward. It might also get my name back in the papers, and that was something I'd wanted for a long time. And since there didn't seem to be any other financial payout coming my way, I deserved at least that much.

I couldn't help feeling like we were grasping at straws, though. The odds against us finding those weapons, or that diamond, were phenomenal. The reality was that in six months, I'd probably have to shave my head and change my name. Even then, it would only be a matter of time. Skully was a true Boss, with tendrils stretching back and forth across the ocean. There wasn't anywhere I could hide from him. Not in another city, not in another country. Maybe I'd buy a cowboy hat and move to Idaho. That might buy me a few months. Or become a carnie and spend the rest of my years traveling the circuit. It couldn't be any weirder than the undercity.

After dropping Gen and Hank downtown, I drove back to Mystic Synergetics. Even though I'd already turned the place inside out once, I figured it was worth double and triple checking. Did I really expect to find something there? No, not really. But I had to do something to keep myself busy while I was waiting for Skully to get out of prison and kill me. Grasping at straws was a better use of my time than meditating on my inevitable demise.

The police tape that had been around the doors at MysticS was gone. The locks had been repaired, and the place was locked up tight. I whipped out my backup set of picks, which I'd picked up before leaving the cabin that morning. I had the door open in five seconds flat.

It was dark and cold inside, not unlike a haunted house in a low budget horror flick, but enough light drifted in from the streetlights that I could easily find my way around. I started my search in the basement. I went through the lockers again, and then searched all the cubbies and drawers in the workstations. When that turned up nothing, I expanded my search to the rest of the building. I went back to the main floor and started digging through the front desk. I found the normal stuff: financial records, employee files, and so on. It wasn't much. Gordy owned MysticS and, as far as I could tell, had never paid a single bill.

He'd leased the building out six months earlier on a credit line. He'd used the same credit line to buy furniture and computers, and to cut paychecks to the business's one legitimate employee, the receptionist. As far as I could tell, the pink-haired gnome girl was the only person who'd made a penny off the entire venture.

Curious as that was, I doubted it made her a suspect. Too many of the pieces had already been fit together, and she had nothing to do with any of them. I realized that the coppers had probably already given her the third degree. If she hadn't said anything yet, she probably didn't know anything. Most likely, Gordy had hired her to give the business the respectable allure he needed to suck Pretty Boy into his scheme. The more I learned about Gordy, the more certain I was that he was nothing but a con artist.

I had to admire him, in a way. He'd figured out what it took to play the game. He'd managed to wrangle himself a genuine white whale. Unfortunately, that whale had killed him before he had reeled the thing in. That's the risk you take when you play in the big pond.

I searched the rest of the building to verify that it was truly as empty as it seemed. It was. That put me right back at square one. I had one last chance: *Maybe* Gordy had stopped by his home before coming back to the lab. He could have stashed the gun there.

I went back to the front desk and pulled Gordy's file. He'd been living in a complex northeast of Downtown. I memorized the address and then called for a cab.

When I pulled up to the place half an hour later, I wasn't surprised to find out it was a real dive. It was a three-story apartment building with peeling paint, old sheets for curtains, and a ramshackle fire escape coming off the back that looked even more dangerous than braving the fire itself. There was a moving truck parked out front, and the front doors were propped wide open. I stepped inside and found myself facing a long hallway lined with doors. A rickety staircase rose up to the right.

I heard voices drifting down from above. I started up the stairs, but then realized the movers were coming down, so I hurried back to the landing to get out of the way. Two burly dwarves wearing jeans and muscle shirts appeared carrying a big screen TV. One of them had a shaved head and a nose ring, the other had long ratty brown hair. They both had numerous tattoos.

"Thanks, buddy," the bald one said.

"Looks like somebody's moving out," I said.

"Moving up's more like it," he replied. "Guy upstairs just won the lotto."

"No kidding?"

"Nope. He says if we have him moved out in two hours, he'll double our fee."

"Good for you," I said. "Better get to work then."

They hurried out to the truck and I started climbing the stairs. I could hear the workers laughing outside as they joked about how they'd spend that big fat paycheck. I wasn't laughing.

I came to Gordy's apartment and found the door open. I peeked inside and saw a dozen boxes of various sizes scattered around the room. I heard a noise to my left and looked over just in time to see a familiar face come walking out of the bedroom. It was a young goblin, and he was wearing a bathrobe and toweling off his hair.

"Don't worry about the kitchen, fellas," he said. "I'll be replacing all that junk."

A FOOL THERE WAS

"Sure thing," I said.

The goblin froze in his tracks. "You!"

I smiled. "I almost didn't recognize you without your bellhop uniform, Wyllem."

He threw the towel down and leapt back into the bedroom. By the time I reached the door, it was locked. I gave it a good hard shove with my shoulder, and it easily popped open. I burst into the room and found him waiting for me, wildly waving a silver wand in my direction.

"Don't come any closer!" he shouted. "I swear, I'll cook you from the inside out."

"Settle down," I said. "I just want you to answer some questions."

The movers reappeared in the living room and started stacking boxes on a dolly. Wyllem motioned for me to sit on the bed. He slid around me and quietly pushed the door shut.

"Okay," he said "By the time you wake up it's not going to make any difference, so I might as well tell you everything. Where do you want me to start?"

"What's your connection with Gordy? Did you kill him?"

"No, I didn't kill him. He was my partner, until he got stupid."

My brain raced, trying to unravel the story we had concocted and rewrite it with this new information. "Gordy was your partner? Then it was the two of you working the con with that machine?"

Wyllem smiled. "It was a perfect plan. It took months to put it all together. See, I'd heard about that diamond of Pretty Boy's. I'd heard Sheba talking about it when she moved into *The Wall*. You wouldn't believe the things people talk about in front of me. It's like they think I'm a robot or something; like they think I can't hear a word they say."

"I see. So you came up with the plan to steal it from Pretty Boy?"

"Of course. I had the whole scheme worked out, top to bottom, but I needed help. It was too much work for one person. I knew Gordy from a previous con job I'd worked, and I needed his expertise. See, he went to engineering college for about six months. He could weld, build computers, just about anything I needed."

"So he built that spider-machine?"

Wyllem laughed loudly. "Brilliant, wasn't it? All we had to do was convince Pretty Boy that we could build a machine that could kill his brother and he'd never get caught. It was supposed to be a spell enhancer, something that could make a spell work from hundreds of miles away. It was ridiculous, of course, but Pretty Boy bought it hook, line, and sinker. That's how bad he wanted to kill his brother."

"Nice family."

"Whatever," he shrugged. "Goblins will be goblins."

"What went wrong? Did Pretty Boy figure out your scam?"

"No, it wasn't that. It was the stupid wife, Nyva. Our plan was working perfectly and then she went and killed Pretty Boy over some stupid affair. She showed up at *The Wall* in tears. I called her sister down, and then escorted them both back upstairs. She blurted out half the story before Sheba even thought to shut her up. Of course by then, I'd already seen the bottle of aspartame."

"So you called off the plan?"

A FOOL THERE WAS

"I didn't have a chance. Pretty Boy was dead, so I had to act fast. I left work early and snuck into Pretty Boy's flat. I knew about the secret entrance, because Sheba had told me all about it. She said that was the way all of Pretty Boy's *friends* snuck in and out. I broke in, and found Pretty Boy dead in his chair, just the way Nyva had left him. I pushed him out of the way so I had some room to work while I broke into the safe."

"And made the switch for a fake diamond?"

"Of course. I had spent a lot of money on that fake. Seven thousand dollars for a *fake* diamond. Can you believe that? But I had to do it. We were going to swap it with the real one when it was time to activate our machine. Thankfully, I'd been carrying the thing with me everywhere I went, because I didn't trust Gordy enough to leave it with him."

"So much trust," I said. "Sounds like a great partnership."

"Sounds like *every* partnership."

"So you stole the real diamond, and left the fake?"

"Of course. After all, I didn't want anyone to come looking for me. At least not right away. But what I didn't know was that Gordy had been following me, because the bastard had been planning to double-cross me all along. When he saw me going into Pretty Boy's building, he knew I was up to something. He must have followed me in while I was snatching the diamond."

"Did he confront you?"

"No, I heard someone coming and hid behind the curtains, but it wasn't Gordy. It was Freddie the Fist. When he came barging in there, I thought I was done for sure. But he took one look at the open safe, grabbed something, and ran off. I wasn't sure what it was, so I looked at the safe on the way out. I didn't see anything missing."

"It was his contract," I said. "Freddie wanted out of his contract, so he stole it."

"And he didn't take anything else?" Wyllem said. "With a safe full of money sitting there, all he took was a piece of paper? What a *mook*."

"No kidding. But what about Gordy? He must have come in right after that."

"Yes, but by then I was gone."

I shook my head in disbelief. "Gordy must have left Pretty Boy's apartment right before I came in," I said.

"You missed Gordy by no more than five minutes. You probably passed him in the lobby. He took the elevator and walked out the front door."

I scratched the stubble on my long, pointy chin. "Hang on a sec. Gordy snuck in after you, but by then, Pretty Boy was already dead. Why did Gordy shoot him?"

"Pretty Boy's back was turned because I had moved the chair getting into the safe. Gordy probably shot him thinking Pretty Boy was still alive. Then he saw the safe standing open, and like the idiot he was, stole the fake diamond."

"That's how Gordy ended up with the fake diamond and Pretty Boy ended up getting murdered twice."

"Exactly."

"After stealing the fake, Gordy went back to the lab, and that's where Skully caught up with him?" I said.

"I suppose so."

I considered that. "What about the gun?"

"Huh?"

A FOOL THERE WAS

"The gun Gordy used to shoot Pretty Boy. I searched that lab twice and couldn't find it anywhere. That's what brought me here."

Wyllem threw back his head and laughed. "Did you check the spider?"

"Eh?"

"The *machine*. You realize that thing's hollow, right? Gordy made it out of old freezer parts. He used to keep his lunch in there."

My jaw dropped open. I had never even considered looking *inside* the spider. Now that I thought about it, it made perfect sense. When I'd found Gordy, his corpse had a sandwich in its pocket. Gordy's *lunch*. He must have taken it out of the freezer to make room for the gun! I smacked myself on the forehead.

"Unbelievable," I mumbled. "So he hid the gun, and put the sandwich in his pocket. Skully must have arrived right after that."

"That's my guess," said Wyllem. "Being the idiot he was, Gordy had set himself up perfectly for the murder *and* the theft. Skully probably realized that and killed him when he took the diamond. The fake diamond, I mean."

"Sounds like Skully," I said with a snort. "And it all worked out in your favor, didn't it?"

"You can say that again. I couldn't have planned this whole thing any better if I'd tried. Hell, if I had *wanted* to pull this off, I'd probably have ended up dead or in prison. After Gordy got killed, I knew there was no way anybody would ever pin it on me, so I threw myself a little party and started planning my move to the big time."

"Unbelievable," I muttered. "All this time ... And Pretty Boy's wives had nothing to do with stealing that diamond."

"Nothing more than the fact that they can't keep their mouths shut."

"I've met Sheba," I said. "That doesn't surprise me."

Wyllem laughed. "Well, I guess that's it," he said, and pointed his wand at me. "You wanna lay down for this?"

I lunged at him across the bed, knocking over his suitcases as I fell. Wyllem stepped to the side and snapped his wand in my direction. A wave of icy energy hit me, and my body instantly began to shake uncontrollably. It was a freezing spell.

I groaned as ice gripped my veins. My heart slowed to a dull thudding in my chest. I could feel my body going rigid, but remained completely consciousness of what was going on. I was just powerless to stop it. Hypothermia took over. I rolled to the side, crashing over the edge of the bed, and landed flat on my back.

Wyllem's face appeared above me. He shook his head, and smiled.

"I'm afraid you've got nothing, Sam. Better luck next time."

With that, he waved the wand one more time and I went completely rigid. I felt my blood turn to ice, my heart struggling in futility to drive the frozen liquid through my veins. My breath froze in my lungs, and my vision clouded over. Then, with one last violent seizure, I lost consciousness.

The spell took two hours to wear off. At least, that was when I finally regained consciousness. It was another twenty minutes before I could move. Even then, I was shaking so violently that all I could do was stand under the warm shower, still fully dressed.

A FOOL THERE WAS

While I was in there, I could hear my phone ringing in the bedroom, where it had fallen from my pocket. I ignored it. It wouldn't have done any good to answer. My voice box was frozen.

When I could finally move my joints, I slipped my hand into the warm, damp pocket of my trench coat and felt the cold unyielding shape of chiseled stone in the palm of my hand. I withdrew the object and held it up to the light, examining the color and clarity, relishing the shape of the water droplets cascading down the brilliant pink facets. I smiled, imagining Wyllem's face as he unpacked his suitcases and found the diamond gone.

I started to laugh...

When I finally felt myself again, I located my cell phone next to the bed and listened to the message. It was Hank:

"Sam, we've searched everything. Gen and I even spent a couple hours interrogating Sheba. We've got nothing. I hope things came out better on your end."

I listened to it three times, wondering what I should do. Part of me wanted to call Hank right back and tell him everything. After Mickey's death, it seemed like he deserved at least that much. Problem was, I was starting to think Hank wasn't such a bad guy. We seemed to have forged some sort of unlikely alliance, and I wasn't sure that was a good thing.

See, I don't like the way extra baggage slows me down. I need to be able to make split decisions. You can't do that when you have to worry about someone else. If you do –if you hesitate- it can cost a whole lot more than a few seconds. That's why I keep my life free of entanglements like friendships and romance. Those things are for chumps, and I ain't no chump.

I pulled the diamond out and looked at it again, still hardly believing I'd pulled it off. Wyllem had made the mistake of his life, leaving that rock in his bags where I could find it. I had a feeling it would be years before he had the guts to show his face in the undercity again.

A goblin could do a lot with a fifteen million dollar rock, I thought.

I had really done it. I'd solved the crime, taken the diamond for myself, and even tricked Wyllem into a confession. I should have been on cloud nine. But for some strange reason, I wasn't. Something was bothering me.

Chapter 18

The guilt was weighing down on me enough that I decided to tell Hank the truth. Most of it, anyway. I found him at the jailhouse under the Mother tree. Gen was there, too. They had given up on trying to wring a confession out of Sheba, which had been complicated by the fact that she was completely innocent. All she had done was try to protect her sister.

I told them about my encounter with Wyllem and the story he'd confessed. I explained how just a minute or two in the timing of events might have entirely changed the course of the story; how I'd missed both Gordy and Wyllem in Pretty Boy's office by no more than five minutes. I told them about Wyllem's source of information, that it had been Nyva herself. And I told Hank where to find the gun. I also broke the bad news that after all I had learned, Wyllem had still managed to escape.

I only left out one tiny, insignificant little detail. After all, what difference did it really make if the diamond was never found? It wasn't like anyone was looking for it. The original owner was dead. Sheba was already filthy rich and Nyva was probably going to prison. They had no claim to it, as far as I could see. The police certainly had no claim either. What business did I have handing it over to the cops?

No, it was best to hang onto it, just for safekeeping. Just for a while...

"It all makes sense," Hank said when I'd finished with my story. "It infuriates me that we don't have anything to convict Skully, but at least we know the truth now."

"He'll slip up eventually," Gen said. "When he does, we'll have him."

"Nothing we do at this point will bring Mickey back," Hank said. "That's the worst part. Even if I track Skully down and rip him apart limb by limb, Mickey will still be dead."

"Give it time, Hank. We'll get him... Oh, Sam, one more thing-" she reached into her pocket and tossed me a set of keys.

"You got my car back?"

"It's in the lot behind the building," she said with a wink. "By the way, you're low on gas."

"Sure I am, dollface. Next time just ask me for a ride."

"Are we still talking about your car?"

"Give me a call and you'll find out."

I left after that. I beat my feet out of there. I hadn't been back to my office in days. I wanted to get home, put on some dry pajamas, and kick my feet up. And a cigar... definitely a cigar.

I had forgotten all about the bomb in my house until I climbed the front stairs and reached for the door handle. Then it all came back to me. It occurred to me that somebody might have put another bomb in there over the last few days. I doubted it, since the first obviously hadn't worked, but you never know what lengths a man like Skully will go to. I decided to play it safe and sneak in the back way, like I had before.

A FOOL THERE WAS

Once I was inside, I searched the place top to bottom, just to be sure. Only when I was finally satisfied that it was safe did I venture back down to my apartment. That was when I saw the stack of mail lying by the front door. I snatched it all up and then climbed the stairs to my office, ready for a bourbon and a cigar.

I was halfway through my smoke when I finally got down to the envelope that I had sent myself. Until that moment, I had completely forgotten about it. I opened it and let the ledger fall to my desk. I exhaled, blowing out a cloud of smoke that billowed across the top of my desk and slowly began to drift, like fog gliding across a moor. Reluctantly, I opened the ledger and began to scan the pages.

At first, nothing seemed that important. I saw payments to fighters like Freddie the fist, who Pretty Boy had bribed to take a fall. Funds transferred from account to account in some sort of laundering scheme. Then I saw something that caught my eye. It was Skully's name.

I scanned the columns and realized I was looking at a document five years old. It must have been before the brothers' falling out, because it documented numerous transactions between Pretty Boy and Skully. They had traded accounts to launder money. They'd set up business fronts for the same purpose, all the while dealing pixie dust, unicorn horns, and other dangerous narcotics.

I set the ledger down and leaned back in my chair, taking a long puff on my cigar. I stared at the thing like it was a rattlesnake, and for good reason. Sure, maybe it was the evidence Hank needed to put Skully away for life. Maybe it was my ticket to a long and healthy life without wincing every time

I started my car or opened my front door... At the same time, it was also solid proof that I'd been in Pretty Boy's apartment on the day of his death, and that I had stolen that ledger from his safe.

Plus, it was worth a huge pile of money. The information in that ledger was priceless. It could be bought, traded, and blackmailed. It was my ticket to the big time. With that information, I could make invaluable friends in the underworld, and I could put enemies behind bars for the rest of their lives. I wasn't sure I was willing to give all that up, just for a little peace of mind. Was I?

Okay, I admit it. I'm a chump. I dumped my cigar in the ashtray, put my coat and hat back on, and drove back uptown.

I didn't just *hand* the ledger to Hank Mossberg, of course. Being the goody-two-shoes he is, he probably would have arrested me for stealing it. Instead, I made sure he'd left for the day and then snuck into his office. I picked the lock on his safe and slid the ledger in, right on top, where he couldn't miss it. Then I locked up and left everything just like it was...

Okay, not *everything*. I couldn't resist it. I had to do *something*. I pulled the lever on his chair, lowering it to within a few inches of the ground. Then I busted off the handle. When Hank sat down in the morning, he'd barely be able to see over his own desk. I may be a pro, but I'm still a goblin. I'm definitely *not* above cheap thrills.

After that, I made one more stop on my way home. I swung by Honey's place. I knew it was a bad idea to be seen hanging around there, especially since her boyfriend was a heavyweight boxing champ, but there had been one more thing nagging at me, and I'd finally figured out what it was.

A FOOL THERE WAS

Honey was home, and so was Freddie. As I mounted the front porch, I could hear the two of them talking in the kitchen. I smelled the heavenly aroma of tortellini al pesto drifting out through the front window, and felt like I was right back in that old kitchen again. Right back in time, right to the beginning of it all.

I sighed quietly, trying to reassure myself that I was doing the right thing. I knocked three times and then vanished into the shadows of the alley across the street before they could reach the door. From my hiding spot, I watched as Freddie opened the door and found no one there. He glanced left and right, narrowing his eyebrows.

"Freddie, who is it?" Honey said. She appeared behind him, peering around his wide shoulders.

"Just a prankster," Freddie said, turning away.

"Wait!" Honey exclaimed. She knelt down and lifted the tiny package I'd left on the floorboards before the door. It was nothing fancy, just a small cardboard box taped shut. They glanced at each other and then opened it, right there in the doorway.

As she pulled back the leaves, Honey caught her breath. She put a hand to her mouth and whispered, "Freddie?"

He reached into the box and pulled out the diamond. He held it in his palm, staring at it. Honey started to cry.

"Oh, Freddie, do you know what this means?"

Freddie closed his fist, glancing nervously up and down the street. He put his arm around Honey and drew her back inside the house. The door closed, and everything became silent. Through the front windows, I saw the two of them embracing, pulling slightly apart to look down at the diamond in Honey's hands, and then drawing back together. They did this several times, as if neither one could believe the strange, wonderful thing that had just happened to them. It would change their lives forever.

I left them to their privacy. I wandered back down the hill, whistling quietly to myself as the sound of my footsteps echoed back and forth between the old brick buildings. A layer of mist hovered overhead, drifting through the upper stories, whitewashing the roof of the cavern.

I didn't consciously pick out a tune, but when I got back to the car, I realized what I had been whistling. It was a very old song, a big band interpretation of an old poem by Kipling, *A Fool There Was*.

He sure got that right. A fool, a sap, a sucker... I was all those things and more. But nobody else had to know. Besides, I didn't need that money as bad as Honey did, and I sure didn't need Skully Marcozi back on the streets.

In this life, you have to play the hand you're dealt, and sometimes playing the fool is almost as good as having an ace up your sleeve.

The End

A note from the author:

Thanks for reading "A Fool There Was." I'm grateful for the opportunity to share my work with you, and for your support. If you wouldn't mind taking a few extra minutes to post a review at Goodreads, Amazon[1], or your favorite e-book website, it would be extremely helpful and very much appreciated. Thanks again, and remember to look for the next book in this series as well as my other titles listed below.

Sign up for my newsletter (click here)[2] for freebies, giveaways, and the latest info on my books, and visit my website[3] for regular updates and *more* free books!

---

1. https://www.amazon.com/dp/B00OQFM1PC

2. https://www.subscribepage.com/i8f0v5

3. http://jamiesedgwick.blogspot.com/

JAMIE SEDGWICK

Text and Artwork Copyright 2014 by Jamie Sedgwick
ISBN-13: 978-0692313923
All rights reserved. Any similarity to real events or people is purely coincidental

Also by Jamie Sedgwick

Aboard the Great Iron Horse
The Clockwork God
Killing the Machine
The Dragon's Breath
Clockwork Legion
Starfall

Hank Mossberg, Private Ogre
Murder in the Boughs
Death in the Hallows
The Killer in the Shadow
A Fool There Was
When the Boughs Break
A Dame to Die For

Shadow Born Trilogy
Shadow Born
Shadow Rising

Shadowlord

The Tinkerer's Daughter
The Tinkerer's Daughter
Tinker's War
Blood and Steam

Standalone
The Darkling Wind
A Fool There Was

Watch for more at www.jamiesedgwick.com.

About the Author

Jeramy Gates is the author of numerous Amazon lists bestsellers in the categories of Mystery, Thriller, Science Fiction and Fantasy (as Jamie Sedgwick). Jeramy spent his childhood on a ranch in the Montana Rockies, but now lives among the grapevines and redwood groves of northern California with his wife and three children. When traveling, you may encounter Jeramy with his family and their three dingoes, camping in their fifth wheel trailer.

Read more at www.jamiesedgwick.com.

Made in United States
Troutdale, OR
12/20/2024

27059009R00152